# FLAWLESS SURRENDER

## THE SURRENDER SERIES 2

### LORI KING

Text Copyright © September 2013 Lori King
Second Edition © February 2015 Lori King
Art and Logo © Copyright Lori King Books
All rights reserved.

Artwork by: Jess Buffett
Jess Buffett Graphic Designs
Published by: Lori King Books

EBooks are not transferrable.
This book is intended for the purchaser's sole use. Sharing, or downloading to other individuals or devices is illegal.
This work is fictional. Any resemblance to real persons, places, or events is purely coincidental. All Rights Are Reserved. No part of this book may be used or reproduced in any manner whatsoever without written permission of the author, except in the case of quotations embodied in critical articles and reviews.

# BLURB

The strength of a man is in the way he embraces his flaws, instead of denying them.

Zoey Carson has worked nonstop to graduate with her Master's degree, after managing to survive parents who neglected her in favor of their own addictions. Her future of helping children overcome their childhood is within her grasp until she is knocked down by a surprise visit from her mother. She finds herself at a crossroads when her longtime crush, Tanner Keegan, comes to her rescue, along with his brothers, Dalton and Clint. Letting them go might help her avoid getting hurt, but the outcome—she would continue to live a lonely, empty life.

The Keegan brothers finally come together after spreading themselves across the globe for more than a decade. Each fighting his own personal battle with the past and future, but there is no question that Zoey turns them all on. Who will risk the pain of baring their soul for the promise of a happy future, and who will succumb to their weaknesses?

Return to Stone River, Texas, where the Keegan brothers work together to win the heart of the woman made for them. Enjoy the journey as Zoey decides if she can be their...Flawless Surrender.

*Warning: For Mature Adult Audiences. Contains language and actions some may deem offensive. Sexually explicit content. M/F/M/M, graphic language, consensual BDSM, spanking, HEA. There is 'No' touching or titillation between siblings.*

*For my children: I hope you will always remember to embrace your flaws,
for that is what makes you uniquely beautiful.
For my husband: You have always accepted and loved me for who I am,
and I love your perfect imperfections.
I hope to always live, laugh, and love like today is my only chance.*

*–Lori*

## ACKNOWLEDGMENTS

*Thank you to Nicole Plummer who helped me name Dalton Keegan, and flesh him out.*

*Thank you to Kerri Good, Tracey Reid, Avery Gale, and Stacey Price who all four shared their creativity with me when I was fantasizing about cowboys.*

# CHAPTER ONE

*The strength of a man is in the way he embraces his flaws instead of denying them.*

Zoey Carson's life was over.

A couple of months ago she received her master's degree and now she would be starting her dream job. In three short weeks, she would be a social worker for the Stone River Junior High School. She would have the opportunity to have an impact on children's lives and perhaps encourage them to reach beyond their circumstances. So how in the world was it possible that everything else in her life fell apart just when she thought she was on the right track?

An hour ago she received the news from her landlord the tiny triplex she had occupied for nearly six years had been sold to a developer and was going to be demolished in thirty days. She lived in Stone River. A tiny two-bit town in bum-fuck Texas where there was a ridiculous shortage of apartments and rental homes for a single woman who didn't have the money to buy a house. So now she was going to be homeless and if the arrival of her mother was any indication, she was going to be broke as well.

Her bone thin, strung out mother stood in front of her with a small backpack flung over her shoulder and a cigarette in her twitchy fingers. Eve Carson only searched her daughter out when she was out of money, or when her latest boyfriend realized what a junkie she really was. Exactly like her ex-husband, Zoey's lame ass father, Andy. They were both worthless, and she counted herself lucky that she hadn't seen her father since she was twelve. She only knew he was still alive because her mother occasionally still hooked up with him to score her next hit. Two adults who never grew up and with no intention of doing so, they had come together in a blaze of passion and ended up with a daughter they didn't know how to take care of and didn't want. Zoey had always been the adult of the family, even as a little girl.

Eve smiled at her as if she was genuinely happy to see her, but Zoey was under no false hopes of a loving reunion. Instead, she had to bite her own tongue to avoid saying something too vicious in greeting.

Propping her hip on the doorjamb, she blocked her mother's entrance into her apartment and crossed her arms over her chest. "Mom? What are you doing here?"

Eve's lips curved up into a tiny smile and Zoey could barely see the faint outline of a bruise marring her jawline. *Uh oh.* That meant she was coming off another bad break up and she was looking for solace.

She was a serial dater and the men she usually kept company with were terrible for her. There had been junkies, drug dealers, abusers, ex-cons, and even a pimp a few years back. It seemed like Eve just knew how to pick the shittiest guys around and fall madly in love with them.

"Do I need a reason to visit my beautiful daughter? I came to say hello and visit with you."

Zoey felt her eyebrow lift nearly to her hairline. "Really? Since when do you randomly drop by Stone River to say hello?"

"Since today, damn it. Now are you going to let your mother in or not?"

Zoey wanted to say no, but she couldn't. Much to her own dismay, she never could deny either one of her parents. Instead, she stepped back and held the door open to her little studio apartment.

Once upon a time, her mother was a beautiful woman, but now her constant battle with alcohol and drugs had taken its toll on her body. She looked emaciated and sick, with a yellowish pallor to her skin. Zoey knew there was a good chance her mother was stoned out of her mind right now, but she gestured to a seat on the couch anyway.

"So, how have you been, Mom?"

"Good, I've been traveling. Leo took me to see Dallas and then San Antonio for a bit. Leo is a great guy. I can't wait for you to meet him. We met down by Galveston when I was looking for work. We had a little spat yesterday, so we're taking a break. Giving each other some space. Since I had nothing else going on right now, I decided it was time for me to come visit my Zoey."

Zoey fought the urge to sigh dramatically. It was just what she expected. "So are you planning on staying for a while?"

Eve's sunken blue eyes widened in a fake act of surprise, "Only if it's not an inconvenience, baby. I wouldn't want to be in your way. I'm sure you have a lot going on right now..."

The words hung there, heavy in the air. Just out of reach. Zoey knew she couldn't say no, so she nodded, "Of course you can stay here. I'm in the middle of looking for a new place to live though."

"Oh? Is this place not good enough for a college graduate anymore?"

Eve stubbed her cigarette out in the houseplant that sat next to the sofa and Zoey had to bite her tongue. "No, Mom. My landlord sold the building. I have a couple of weeks to figure out where I'm going to move.

"I see, well I won't concern myself with the details. I'm sure you will work it all out. What else have you been up to, baby? It's been months since we sat down and chatted. Do you have a man yet? I met Leo at a bar. He was singing in a local band, and one look was all it took. We've been wandering around the state of Texas together, a little like nomads, but you know I enjoy traveling. Do you have anything to eat? I skipped breakfast this morning, and I'm starving now."

Zoey bit her tongue to keep from responding to Eve's rush of words. This was the way she was. It was Eve's world and Zoey felt like she was caught up in a hurricane when she was around, flung about without a handhold. Walking into the kitchen, she tugged the fridge door open and began pulling out the things she would need to throw together a quick sandwich for her mom. Within moments, Eve had two sandwiches and a bag of chips in front of her, happily chattering away about Leo and their misadventures all over the Lone Star state.

"I'm sorry, baby, I've been yapping away at you and I haven't even given you a chance to talk! Now that you're done with school, what do you plan to do?

Zoey hesitated to be sure the Eve-storm was over before she responded. "I got a job with the local school district. I start in a couple of weeks."

"Really? I guess nowadays with all of the school shootings and stuff it makes sense they would want head doctors in the schools." The solemn look on Eve's face had Zoey shaking her head.

"I'm not a head doctor, Mom. I'm a licensed social worker."

Eve shrugged. "Same diff. I mean really, you listen to crazy self-centered folks all day long and make them feel better about themselves, right?"

Zoey took a deep breath to calm her nerves and pinched the bridge of her nose as she fought back a snarky reply. "Mom, I've got to go out for a bit. Will you be okay here by yourself?"

"Oh sure! I think I'll indulge in a nice long shower and then maybe take a nap. I haven't slept much either lately."

Her mom pulled another cigarette from her purse and reached for her lighter.

"Please, Mom, not in here. You know I can't stomach the smell."

Eve rolled her eyes and her lip curled up in a half smile-half cringe. "Yeah, you always were sensitive about things like that. I'll take a quick walk downstairs and be back in a flash."

While her mom was gone, Zoey cleaned up the mess left behind in the kitchen, and slid her feet into a pair of sandals. She had her purse over her shoulder and her keys in hand as she crossed paths with Eve going to her car. She had a feeling she was going to be spending a lot more time out of her home rather than trapped inside with her mom.

After a quick text to her best friend, Rachel, as she was starting her beat up four-door sedan, she was on the road with all four windows down and the stifling summer heat of Texas blasting through her dark hair. Oddly enough, even the heavy humid air didn't stop her from inhaling deeply and sending up a prayer of thanks for the distance she had come since her parents split. She was a grown ass woman with ambitions and goals and her mother was not going to get in her way. Being homeless however, might pose a problem.

Kasey Musgraves new song "Blowing Smoke" echoed over her stereo as she rounded the long dirt drive up to Rachel's home. Brooks Pastures was one of the most prominent ranches around Stone River and the four Brooks brothers had made up the majority of the towns hottest bachelors list until last summer.

Rachel managed to land all four brothers in one fell swoop, shocking the town and making history. Zoey had braced for some flare-ups about the new polyamorous relationship but oddly, the whole town seemed to embrace the happy family and congratulate them as one. The fact they had just had a beautiful bouncing baby girl might have helped that a little.

Juliet was the sweetest little cherub Zoey had ever seen, and every time she was near the little girl, it was as if her womb clenched. She wanted a baby of her own desperately, but at the moment, the lack of male companionship posed a serious problem. She had been so focused on her career goals that she had put every other need aside, and besides the occasional hot and sweaty hookup that left her wanting, she hadn't really had a serious relationship. She craved cuddling, and the intimacy and affection that went with a serious relationship. Someday she wanted just one man to look at her and want her from the top of her dark hair to the bottom of her ridiculously oversized feet.

Rachel was waiting on the front porch with a tall glass of sweet tea and a chocolate candy bar when Zoey parked and jumped out. It was just the sort of thing that Zoey needed and she hurried up the steps into her best friend's arms.

"I'm so glad you're not back to work yet," she mumbled into Rachel's shoulder.

"Me too. It sounded like an urgent situation. What the hell is your mom doing back in Stone River?" Zoey took a step back and accepted the sweet treat from Rachel before following her into the house.

"She's here to crash at my place because she ran out of money and her newest man, Leo, wouldn't take care of her anymore. I can't tell if she's strung out yet, but she's sporting a fading bruise on her jaw that she didn't give to herself."

"Who has a bruise?" Parker Brooks stepped into the living room just as they were settling onto the sofa.

"My mom. She showed up at my place after another bad break up. I'm stuck with her until she gets bored of Stone River again." Zoey let out a dejected sigh as she took a big bite of chocolate and let it melt on her tongue. It was amazing how much chocolate could do for a girl in need.

"Why don't you just tell her to get her own place?" Parker asked, bending and pressing a quick kiss to Rachel's lips before he sat down in a chair nearby. His jeans and button down shirt were covered in dust, and there was a streak of grime on his cheek making him look like the consummate cowboy.

"Because she has no money. She never has any money, mostly because she spends it all on alcohol or cocaine," Zoey's sarcastic comment didn't cover up the hurt in her tone, and she looked down into her glass of sweet tea, blinking rapidly to keep tears back.

"The guys don't know about your mom, Zoey, I didn't think it was my place to tell them." Rachel was looking at her with pity, and if there was anything Zoey despised, it was pity.

Too many adults looked at her with pity over the years, supposedly sympathizing with her plight, while standing by and allowing it to continue. Her parents never hit her, or physically abused her in a way that would be punishable by law, but they sure were good at neglecting her.

She could remember countless mornings waking up shivering in a house with no heat in the dead of winter, or taking a bath in the creek behind her house because the water had been shut off. The kids at school didn't know the extent of her situation, but they knew she wore grimy clothes that didn't fit right. So she became an outcast. Finding Rachel in the second grade was the only good thing that had happened to Zoey in her whole childhood. Rachel's parents had just split up, and her father had run off to another state with his secretary leaving his family behind. The gossip and chatter put Rachel on the outcast list too, and they connected.

"My mom wasn't a good mom, and for that matter, my dad was pretty shitty too. It's not a big deal."

Rachel and Parker exchanged a look, and for one brief moment Zoey was afraid Rachel would say more, but Parker seemed to shut her down with one of his "don't mess with me" looks. Instead, Rachel turned and asked her, "So what is this about a developer?"

"Oh yes, that's the other big news. Langley gave me notice this morning that he sold the house to that developer who just moved here. I don't remember her name, but she is planning on tearing the place down and building a small sub-division. Apparently the folks in the city like the idea of small town living—as long as they get to keep their suburban housing. So I will be out of a place to live in four weeks, no matter what."

Zoey let her head fall back on the sofa and closed her eyes. Saying it out loud made it all the more real.

"Shi-oot." Rachel corrected herself before she cursed in front of Parker, and Zoey looked up just in time to catch the heated look the two lovers shared. "You can always stay here, girl. Now that the remodeling is done on the Master Suite we have a guest bedroom."

"Um, only one? Didn't this house have four bedrooms before?" Zoey asked with a raised eyebrow.

Parker chuckled and Rachel snorted before explaining. "I have four husbands, but there is only one of me. So two guys per night can share the bed. That means the other two are on their own, and Juliet has her own room. That leaves one guest bedroom."

Zoey was instantly sorry she asked as images of her best friend and her four scorching hot husbands sharing a bed and other activities filled her brain. "God, I'm sorry. That was insanely rude of me to ask."

Parker just laughed while Rachel waved it off. "No biggie. No reason to lie about it. Besides, these guys are taking their lives into their own hands every time they sleep next to me. I kick like a donkey."

"That ain't no shit," Parker muttered under his breath and then grimaced when Rachel cleared her throat. "Sorry, it slipped out. You know Zoey, Tanner Keegan has a room open right now. In fact, he was just saying the other night at Robin's that he was going to be looking for a renter soon. It's the room over the garage I believe. Like an apartment type thing. You should call him."

Zoey's stomach clenched. Sure, that was easy for Parker to say. If he knew the history between her and Tanner, he never would have suggested such a ridiculous plan.

Tanner Keegan was the only man currently residing in Stone River who could make her blood boil with just his presence. Her vagina wanted him more than anything else, but she had already tried to walk that road once.

Zoey had basically thrown herself at Tanner several years ago, and he had bluntly rejected her, telling her that he only took women to bed, not little girls. It had left her self-esteem shattered, and her ego squashed. No. No way was she ever going to let that man have that kind of control on her life again. Besides, it was highly unlikely Tanner would ever consider allowing her to rent the room from him. When she was around, he acted as if she had leprosy or something twisted and contagious. Stephen King couldn't have written a better story of avoidance and horror than the relationship she had with Tanner Keegan.

"Uh-no, thanks anyway. I'm sure I'll find something acceptable within the next month." She looked down at the empty chocolate wrapper she was twisting in her fingers rather than meet Parker's curious gaze.

"Tanner would rent it to you at a fair price. His brother, Dalton, do you remember him?" When Zoey nodded silently, Parker continued, "That was his place until he left for medical school. Hasn't been back in ten years. Tanner has rented it out a few times to make extra money when the cash flow isn't as high. With that drought last season, everyone's pinching pennies this season."

Zoey felt like a cornered rabbit. How was she supposed to explain to Parker why she couldn't be around Tanner? Not to mention how her pussy clenched at the mention of the beautiful God-like Dalton, who she hadn't seen in a decade. "Actually, Tanner and I aren't the best of friends."

Parker looked surprised right before his eyes narrowed and he did that weird Alpha male thing where he looked down his nose at her and made her feel about two inches tall. "Zoey Carson, I've never known you to be afraid in your life."

"I'm not afraid of him!" she blustered vehemently. "I just don't want to subject myself to his presence any more than necessary. I will start apartment hunting as soon as I can push my mom out the door and send her back to her newest fuck toy."

"No cursing," Parker commanded and Zoey rolled her eyes. The hard glare he gave her had her shrugging and apologizing pretty quickly. "First of all the word sounds terrible coming from a beautiful woman, and second, my Jules doesn't need to be exposed to that."

Rachel snorted, "Yeah, because you and your brothers never curse around her, right?"

Parker had the grace to look admonished. "Occasionally, but we're trying to curb it."

"I promise, Parker, I will do my best when I'm here or around Juliet to tame my terrible language," Zoey said, not wanting to be on his bad side for any reason. Ridiculous or not.

"Thank you. Now, ladies, if you will excuse me, I need to get back to the barn. It was good to see you, Zoey, and if you change your mind about asking Tanner, well, let's just say I would trust that man with my own daughter. He would never do you harm."

Zoey couldn't hold his gaze so she just nodded and looked back to Rachel hoping Parker would take the dismissal and let the subject go. She sighed with relief when the front door shut behind him.

"Well, that was a pretty intense reaction to a harmless solution," Rachel said, eyeballing Zoey.

"Harmless? Do you remember what happened between Tanner and me? That wasn't harmless. I got kicked in the gut," Zoey said, belligerently swirling her ice in her empty tea glass.

Rachel was quiet for a moment. "Zoey, you've seen him around town, and he's never been anything but respectful. Surely you don't still hold a grudge?"

"So you're telling me that when you see Mitch Edwards and his new fiancée, Connie, that you don't want to punch him in his overly white toothy smile?"

Zoey smirked when Rachel's eyes darkened and her eyebrow rose. "That is totally different."

"I don't see how. I offered Tanner Keegan my body and my heart and he stomped on it with his boot heel. I have no intention of making myself vulnerable around him again." Standing abruptly, she waved her glass at Rachel. "Now, is there anymore tea, or do I need to run to the store for emergency rations?"

## CHAPTER TWO

An hour later, Zoey and Rachel were sprawled out on the front porch with empty glasses and ice cream bowls that were nearly licked clean, when a sudden thumping music grabbed their attention. A cloud of red dust rose in the air down the road. That could only mean someone was coming down the driveway in their direction.

"Who's that?" Zoey asked, deciding it didn't really matter to her that much as long as she didn't have to move. Rachel's porch was absolutely perfect for relaxing on a late summer afternoon. It was wide with deep steps that suited Zoey's wide ass to a T, and it had a slew of inviting rocking chairs, and flower baskets scattered all over it. Heaven on Earth was drinking sweet tea while having girl talk on the front porch.

"I have no idea. The guys have people out here all of the time to look at the horses though, and we have some yearlings that are ready to be sold. Could be a client." Rachel shifted so her feet were on the floor instead of hanging over the arm of the rocking chair she sat in, but otherwise she didn't move to go greet the visitor.

As a dark red pickup truck came into view, the sound of Tim McGraw's "Truck Yeah" thumped through the air. Zoey's heart skipped a beat and her stomach tightened. That red truck was familiar.

When the vehicle finally came to a stop in the driveway about thirty yards from them, Zoey's eyes met the drivers and she gasped. No way. It couldn't be.

Tanner Keegan in all of his male glory stepped from the truck. His six foot tall muscular cowboy frame was encased in a pair of worn Wranglers and a faded black t-shirt that hugged his tight abs like a second skin. Atop his head sat a black cowboy hat that shaded his gorgeous amber colored eyes from her view. Her eyes ate him up as always, until he turned to face them and headed their way.

*Damn. Did he catch her staring?*

"Hey, ladies."

"Tanner, this is a surprise. What are you doing so far from home?" Rachel asked calmly. Zoey's eyes narrowed in on Rachel's face and she wondered if this was a set-up of some sort.

No, her friend knew how she felt about Tanner. She wouldn't do that. It had to be some sort of odd coincidence.

"Parker said you have some new foals, and we've been talking about coordinating our breeding programs. Ideally it will make us all money when we have stronger stock." Zoey could feel Tanner's gaze, but she kept her eyes half closed where she lay slumped on the porch steps trying to keep her breathing and heart rate calm. "Hey, Zoey. Long time no see."

She had to swallow hard to avoid saying something snarky about their last face to face encounter. "Hi, Tanner, how are you?"

"Really good. Staying busy. I heard you graduated?"

He leaned against the post right next to her, so she was forced to look all the way up his sexy frame from a very bad angle. Trying to stop a blush from climbing her cheeks, she threw a glance at Rachel hoping her friend would help her. Instead, Rachel sat there looking like nothing was wrong. Completely relaxed.

*Bitch.*

"Yeah, just a couple of months ago. I'll be working at the Stone River Junior High School."

Juliet chose that moment to wake from her nap and let out a loud cry so Rachel had to jump up and excuse herself, leaving Zoey to face her dream guy all by herself. It was an awkward sort of nightmare.

Tanner cleared his throat when silence ensued. Zoey shifted on the step so she was sitting up a little more and facing to the side instead of directly at his crotch. The tension was thick, and she didn't know what to do about it.

When Tanner shifted his stance once more, she sighed. There was no way to avoid someone who was two feet away. "So how is the ranch doing?"

His lip lifted in a half smile and she had the idea that he was pleased she broke first. "Good, but the drought hurt us. Last season's stock didn't fatten or strengthen the way they should have. That's why the guys and I are discussing partnering up our horse breeding programs."

"If the Triple T and Brooks Pastures are working together, it's a guaranteed success," she said, and she had to hold in a moan when his lips spread into a wider smile.

"Thank you for that vote of confidence. I think so too."

"So how is your family? Do your parents like living in Arizona?"

Tanner's parents had retired to Arizona a couple of summers before, turning the running of the ranch over to Tanner alone. Zoey knew Tanner was the oldest of the Keegan boys, and the only one who seemed interested in ranching. Dalton was a doctor working in some far off country helping the needy, and Clint had run off right out of high school to become an actor in California. All three of them were older than Zoey and Rachel. Clint was five years older making him thirty this year, and that would put Tanner at about thirty-three.

"Mom loves it, pops misses home. They are planning to come home for a visit at Christmas. The retirement community has been good for mama though. She spends her time with her friends keeping active." Tanner moved to sit on the step next to her, and she felt goose bumps pop up on her arms.

"Hmm...yeah, I can't imagine your dad slowing down." Zoey shifted away just a little bit trying to put more distance between them. Tanner's eyes narrowed just a bit but he didn't comment.

"He really didn't have a choice after the heart attack."

She felt her mouth fall open, "Your dad had a heart attack? When?"

His jaw tightened and he grimaced, "Yeah, it was about six months before they decided to retire. It damaged his heart quite a bit, so Doc said he needed to slow it down and take it easy. Before that, it never seemed possible that pops was a mere mortal. Working sun up to sun down without a vacation or a rest...well, I guess we're all only human, right?"

Zoey's heart lurched in her chest, and she reached out her hand to cover his fist on his thigh before she could stop herself. "I'm sorry, Tanner. I can only imagine how hard it must be to see him growing older and weaker. At least he survived the heart attack and you have more time with him."

---

Tanner's mind went blank the moment Zoey's skin touched his. If he was honest, he had been struggling to think ever since he turned the bend and saw her sexy body stretched out on the porch steps. She looked like a fifties pin-up in cut off blue jeans and a blue tank top that made her ocean blue eyes look dark and mysterious. Her jet black hair hung in a solid sheet of straight satin down her back, and he ached to wrap it around his fist and pull her up against him.

He was all too aware of the fact that his own mouth ruined his chances with Zoey Carson. When she made a play for him at Robin's all those years ago, he had assumed she was joking. She was only twenty at the time, and to his twenty-eight-year-old mind, that had been an incomprehensible situation. She was naïve, and way too innocent for a kinky pervert like him, so he did what was right instead of what his cock wanted, and he shut her down. If only he had found a more delicate way of doing it, maybe they could have had a chance later.

Shaking off his wandering mind and his dirty thoughts, he pulled his brain back into the moment.

"Thanks. I've adjusted. I had to hire a few hands to help on the ranch, but otherwise everything kept moving forward just like always."

He ached to turn his hand over and link his fingers through hers. What would she say? Would she freak out, or get angry? Knowing Zoey, she would punch him in the nose.

Abruptly she stood, giving him and eyeful of her sexy legs, and her sweetly curving backside. Her hips were made for a man to hold onto, and his cock wanted him to be that man.

"I better say my goodbyes and get home. It will be dark soon."

Tanner stood and turned to face her. He was two steps down from her, so their faces were nearly level, and his eyes zeroed in on her mouth out of habit. Her lips parted and he saw her sharp intake of breath as she swayed on her feet slightly. It took all of his strength to shove his hands in his pockets and step to the side breaking the tension.

A sharp whinny followed by a man's howl of pain startled them both, and Tanner stopped thinking. He turned on his boot heel and ran for the barn. It wasn't until he skidded to a stop and felt Zoey plow into the back of him that he realized she followed. His arm went out to instinctively catch her up against him so she wouldn't fall, and her hands caught his waist clutching at his t-shirt.

The erection in his pants wasn't deterred one iota by the terrible scene in front of him. Sawyer Brooks was sprawled out on his back in the middle of the barn alley, one leg twisted at a disturbing angle, and blood running down his face.

"Sweet Jesus! Sawyer, what the hell happened?"

"I'll go call for help!" Zoey said, and Tanner gave her a nod as he dropped to his knees next to his friend. She was out the door in a flash, her black hair swinging behind her.

Sawyer groaned, "I was saddling that new mare we just got, Clover, and she got spooked by something. When I tried to calm her down she started bucking and kicking to get away from me. She kicked me clear across the barn and I felt my knee pop before it twisted underneath me."

Tanner looked up when Parker ran into the barn from the corral entrance. "Damn, Sawyer! What the hell did you do to yourself? I just saw Clover shoot out of the barn and figured something was wrong."

"Stupid fucking horse, whose dumbass idea was it to buy that one?" Sawyer's face was pale and his jaw was clenched with pain as he reached up to his forehead to feel the wound.

Parker grunted, "I hate to say it, but it was yours."

Sawyer cursed again, and made a move to sit up only to let out a groan of pain when his bent leg shifted.

"Stay put until the ambulance gets here. You've done something bad to that knee, and if you try to move you might make it worse." Tanner looked around for something to press on Sawyer's bloody head to stop the bleeding. In the end, he just tugged his own t-shirt off and pressed it to his friend's forehead. "This cut will need stitches too. I can see your skull, but lucky for you, not your brain."

Parker snorted, but his face remained drawn with tension. "He has no brain to see. Sawyer, I thought we agreed to wait on Clover's training until we could put her through her paces together a few times?"

"Yeah, well you were busy, and I had time to work on it today. We needed to get her going," Sawyer said, groaning when Tanner moved and brushed his injured leg.

"It's not like I expected her to freak out like that."

The barn door creaked loudly as it was thrown open and Rachel came barreling in with a bundle full of blankets and baby. Her eyes widened in horror as she took in the situation. Tanner watched a myriad of emotions cross her face before she set her jaw in determination and nudged him out of his place next to her husband.

"Sawyer Brooks, what have you done to yourself? Have you lost your mind getting hurt? This will not, I repeat, will not get you out of changing diapers, do you hear me?"

Tanner was stunned to find her pushing the infant into his arms so she could focus on Sawyer's injuries. For a heart stopping moment, his inner bachelor freaked out at the tiny bundle of future he held in his big hands, but with everyone focused on Sawyer, he was able to get his nerves under control pretty quickly. Rising to his feet, he stared down at the little girl and he was pleased to see her smiling back at him. She really was adorable.

Rachel and Parker were taking care of Sawyer, so Tanner backed up and took a seat on a stack of hay bales holding Juliet close to his naked chest so he wouldn't accidentally drop her. It was then that he noticed Zoey standing nearby watching him with a smile on her face.

"What?" he asked with a frown. Juliet seemed to sense the change in his mood because she whimpered a little, triggering an instant shushing sound from his mouth and a little bouncing movement from his arms. He hadn't even known he could do that.

Zoey moved closer and reached out to stroke her finger over Juliet's tiny fist. The fingers stretched out and then curled around her index finger like a cuff linking the three of them.

"I've never seen you holding a baby before. You seem to be a natural." Tanner lifted his eyes to hers and he was surprised to see longing in their depths. It must be a female thing to find men holding babies sexually attractive because Tanner didn't feel sexy in the least. However, he wanted Zoey just as much as her blue eyes seemed to want him, so it made for an awfully fascinating cluster fuck of feelings in his chest.

"This is the first time I've held one in years. I didn't even hold her when she was born." He heard the words coming out of his mouth, but he wasn't in control of them.

Zoey glanced back over her shoulder as the sound of an ambulance siren wailed down the drive to the house.

"You've done a bang up job on yourself, Brooks." Silas White was an old school mate of the guys, and Tanner was actually relieved to see him and his partner coming through the door. There was no better paramedic than Silas.

Within moments they were assessing Sawyers injuries and relaying information back to the 911 operator. Somehow in those brief seconds, Zoey had managed to plant herself right in front of Tanner like a human shield between the tiny being in his arms and the painful situation for her father.

"Is he going to be okay, Si?" Rachel asked from her place against Parker's chest. Despite her initial confidence, the pallor of her skin proved she was freaking out like the rest of them.

Silas looked up at her with a smile, "Of course he is, Rachel, but he's going to have to go to the hospital in Austin. If I were to hazard a guess, I would say he's torn something in that knee. We can patch up his head and give him something for pain at the clinic, but then we'll have to transport him to have an MRI done."

Rachel looked up at Parker and then back at Sawyer before her eyes landed on Tanner and her daughter. "I can't leave Juliet."

"Yes you can, I'll watch her," Zoey responded firmly, and just like that, the tiny woman took control of the situation. "I'll stay here with Jules, while you two go to the hospital with Sawyer. Where are Rogan and Hudson at?"

Parker's eyes came up to meet hers, and Tanner could see the concern in his glazed expression. "Austin. They went to take care of some business and won't be back until late. They can meet Rachel at the hospital. I still have the evening chores to do and the animals can't wait, but I would be grateful if you could stay to watch Jules."

"I'll stay with them so you can go, Parker. You need to be with Rachel and Sawyer, and I can handle your evening chores." The words spilled off Tanner's tongue before he could stop them, and the relief on Rachel's face was blinding.

Zoey frowned, and for just a moment Tanner wanted to laugh at the annoyance on her face. So Miss Carson didn't want to spend the evening with him. Well that was certainly a change from her words years ago. He wondered if he could change her mind.

"Thank you, Tanner!" Rachel said, pausing just long enough to press a kiss to her daughter's forehead before she followed Sawyer and the paramedics out of the barn.

Parker stepped over and ran his finger over Juliet's tiny head. "Thank you both. Rachel looks like she's keeping her cool, but she's falling apart inside. Knowing you guys have it under control will keep her a little calmer. Oh, and Tanner, you can help yourself to a shirt when you get in the house."

He tipped his hat at Zoey and then disappeared out the door leaving Tanner and the two females alone listening to the sounds of vehicles leaving.

"Well that was a lot of excitement for one day," Zoey said with a heavy sigh.

Tanner watched her as she pinched the bridge of her nose. "He'll be okay, you know. If it's torn they might have to do surgery, but it will heal up in a couple of weeks."

Zoey's smiled tightly, "Yeah, I know you're right. I guess we better get Juliet back inside before it gets much darker."

Tanner glanced toward the corral doors to find the sun was almost completely set already. "Alright, you take her and I'll get the chores done as quickly as possible." He passed Zoey the baby. Her gasp startled him, but the heat in her eyes as she stared at his naked chest had his cock hard as iron behind his zipper. Her gaze stroked over his wide shoulders to his light pink nipples and followed the line of dark hair that split his pecks and led the way to the waistband of his jeans. The moment her view tipped to stare at the bulge behind the denim, he stopped breathing.

Zoey still wanted him.

There was no denying the flames in her blue eyes, or the flush that crept up her high cheekbones, and inside he was a mass of confusion. Physically, he wanted to eat her up. To fuck her until she was hoarse from screaming his name. But nothing had changed. He was still too old for her, and way too perverted. Hell, the first time he told her to get to her knees and suck his cock, she would probably bite it off. No, Zoey wasn't for him. No matter how much they physically set each other on fire.

He cleared his throat, and her blush darkened. "I better grab a shirt first. Can you manage her without me for a bit?"

Zoey tossed that curtain of black hair arrogantly and glared at him. "For your information I've been babysitting since I was twelve. I can handle one tiny human without your assistance, Superman."

"Good, because I left my cape at home," he called out as she left with Juliet clutched to her shoulder. Tanner sat for a moment in the cooling evening air willing his erection away before he went into the house to grab a shirt. The sounds of Zoey cooing to Juliet in the nursery burned into his brain and made his hard heart clench.

He had already decided that Zoey wasn't for him. Now he just needed to keep his distance. Even as he thought it, his inner voice scoffed.

---

Zoey watched Tanner talking with the baby as if she was a regular little person and might respond back at any moment. Laughter built in her chest, overwhelming her discomfort at being alone with her dream guy. This wasn't how she had intended the rest of her day to go, but then her day had been pretty fucked up from the beginning, so what difference did it make at this point.

"Are you going to stand over there all evening and just watch from a distance?"

Her head popped up and her blue eyes clashed with his in surprise and irritation. "I was just enjoying your rather adult conversation with an infant who hasn't even found her toes yet."

"Sure she has. She was sucking on them earlier. Weren't you Julie?" Tanner bent his head and pressed a sweet kiss to the little girl's tiny foot.

"You do realize that I would be fine with her by myself, right? You've already done the chores, so if you need to leave..."

"Are you trying to get rid of me?"

"Well, no, but I know how busy you are."

Tanner's lip curled up in a smile. "Do I make you nervous, Zoey?"

Zoey just snorted, refusing to respond to the question, but it seemed to please Tanner more.

"Good, I like knowing I keep you a little off balance. You seem to rock my world every time you get close to me." Tanner spoke the words as he continued to play with the baby, and Zoey stared at him in shock.

"What?"

"Oh don't play the innocent. You're standing just out of reach, so I can't accidentally touch you because you know that if I get my hands on you, you'll come undone." His tone changed and when he turned his head to stare at her pointedly, she could see his eyes were darker and his nostrils were flaring. He really was affected by her. It was a stunning revelation and one she wasn't exactly sure she was ready to handle. "Don't worry, I agree it's probably for the best."

Pain lanced through her heart, and she was reminded of the embarrassment and shame she felt when she approached him years ago. Stiffening her spine and tipping her head, she snapped at him. "I'm going to go see if there is something in the kitchen I can throw together for dinner while you keep her occupied." Zoey spun on her heel and scurried away from the scene of domesticity that she craved more than anything else in the world.

She couldn't watch Tanner playing with baby Juliet and not crave him. It wasn't possible. So it was just better if she kept her distance. She could be civil for a couple of hours and then avoid him forever. Maybe she should rethink this living and working in Stone River plan.

Zoey managed to put together the ingredients for omelets pretty easily and before long she had two plates of fluffy eggs, ham and cheese ready to serve. Warming a bottle, she headed into the living room to find her charge.

Tanner was lying on his side on the floor dangling a pretty pink and purple butterfly toy over Juliet, whose chubby legs and bare toes kicked for all she was worth. Her eyes weren't even really focused on the toy, but he seemed to be enjoying their playtime. She almost hated to interrupt. Her eyes skimmed down the length of his long body, from the top of his buzzed hair to the bottom of his now bootless feet. He had a wide back that narrowed into a tight ass, and his legs looked a mile long in those faded blue jeans. If she wasn't a lady, she would do terrible, nasty things to him like her pussy wanted her too.

As if sensing her, Tanner glanced over his broad shoulder and winked. "Hey, sweet cheeks, stop staring at my ass."

She gasped and felt heat creep up over her cheeks. "What? I wasn't!"

"Really?"

Juliet started to fuss and Zoey remembered the bottle in her hand. "I've got a bottle for her, and I have food ready for us if you're hungry."

Tanner climbed to his feet in a swift, gracefully sexy motion that reminded Zoey of a tiger slinking through a forest. "Are you hungry Julie-girl? Auntie Zoey wants to feed us, so best get our butts in there. I haven't eaten a home-cooked meal for weeks."

Zoey laughed as she turned to lead the way into the kitchen, "Well it's not fine dining, just omelets."

She stopped next to the dining table, but Tanner continued to move toward her with the baby in his arms. He slowed just inches away, staring into her eyes. "If you cooked them for me, I can't believe they are *just* anything."

Her voice box wouldn't work, so they just stood there, staring at each other. However, Juliet wasn't patient as she started fussing about her hungry belly. Zoey reached for her and tried not to think about the warmth of the man who brushed her fingers. Shushing the baby, she lifted the bottle for her, pleased when Juliet took it easily. Cradling her against her breasts, she sighed as the scent of sweet baby filled her nose.

Tanner still stood there watching them, and when Zoey looked back up at his face, she could have sworn there was a deeper emotion etched into his smile. It was gone in a flash, and he gestured for her to take a seat.

"So how are you going to eat and feed her at the same time?" he asked as he carried their two plates over to the kitchen table, and then searched out two glasses for tea.

"If I told you I would have to kill you," Zoey joked, and Tanner's immediate frown had her laughing. "Women have some sort of innate ability to multitask. We'll be just fine. Can you pass me the salt though?"

Tanner handed her the tiny glass jar and Zoey flinched when electricity seemed to skitter from her fingertips up her arm and into her brain. He settled into his seat as though nothing had happened so she decided to just ignore it. His loud groan was her reward for the time spent cooking as he took a large bite of the steaming egg mixture.

"I'll take that as a compliment," she said with a smirk on her face as she tucked Juliet's bottle under her chin and proceeded to take a bite of her own meal.

"Damn, woman, if I had known you could cook like this I might have kidnapped you and kept you chained in my kitchen," he said between bites. Heat spiked in her veins and she had to remind herself that he didn't know she liked bondage, so it wasn't a come-on.

"I'm glad you like it. I don't get the chance to cook for other people very often, but I enjoy it." She took another bite and then sighed heavily. "I suppose I'll get to cook a lot more until my mom goes back to wherever she's been."

Tanner looked up in surprise, "Your mom? What's she doing in Stone River? I thought she left after the Sherriff arrested her for causing a nuisance."

Zoey grimaced remembering the incident in question. Tanner and the Sherriff were the only two people besides Zoey and Eve who knew about that terrible evening. Eve had been on a bender and managed to drive Zoey's car into a ditch between the Triple T ranch and town. Tanner had been the first one on the scene and he had been the one to pull her unconscious mom from the car. She still remembered the pity on his face at the scene when she explained how her mom was passed out drunk and not actually hurt.

"Yeah, she left for a bit, but she appeared on my doorstep this afternoon. I'm stuck with her until she decides to move on, or until I get evicted." She took another bite of food, but it didn't taste nearly as appetizing anymore. Dropping her fork, she shifted the baby to the middle of her chest and dropped a quick kiss to her tiny forehead.

When she looked up, Tanner was watching her with an odd look on his face. "Can't you just tell her she's not welcome?"

"Would you be able to tell Dalton or Clint that, if they showed up tomorrow at your door? She's family. Anyways, it won't take long before she's bored with Stone River again and moves on."

Tanner went back to eating and the only sound for a few minutes was the clink of a fork against a plate. When he had nearly licked his plate clean he settled back into his chair and ran his hand over his flat stomach.

"That was the best meal I've had in months. Thank you."

Zoey laughed, "You're welcome, but honestly it wasn't much. You should try my French Toast, that's heaven on earth."

Tanner's eyes flashed, "Was that an invitation to breakfast?" Zoey's mouth dropped open and her heart skipped a beat, but Tanner took mercy on her and let it drop. "So tell me why you would get evicted? Because of your mom?"

"No, Carl Langley sold several of his properties to that new developer. Schmidt Properties or something like that. They are going to tear down the old houses and build new ones." Zoey watched as Tanner stretched his thick arms up and over his head until he was bracing his neck. At that angle he looked arrogantly sexy, and she wanted to lick her way from his perfect lips down to his lean hips.

"So where does that leave you?"

"On the streets if I don't find a new place I guess. I just found out today, so I haven't really figured it all out yet." Looking down, she realized Juliet had drifted off to sleep and the bottle was now just resting in the corner of her mouth, milk dribbling down her tiny chin. "I better get her into bed. Do you mind clearing away the dishes? I'll come wash them in a minute."

Tanner shook his head no, "Go put her to bed and then sit down in the living room. You cooked, I'll clean up. I might just be a backwoods rancher, but I have a few manners left in me."

She let out a laugh as she took the baby to bed, refusing to acknowledge the warmth building in her belly. Just being around him felt right, and this whole playing house scene did nothing to curb the longing she felt. She was going to have to get a grip on herself, before she got hurt again.

Once Juliet was settled, Zoey flipped on the TV and stretched out on the sofa. Tanner reappeared wiping his hands on his jeans. "Kitchen's cleaned up. Thank you again for cooking for me." He flopped down on one of the chairs and rested his sock covered feet up on the coffee table, making himself at home.

"Anytime," she responded without even thinking and immediately wanted to kick herself.

"So, I was thinking, I have Dalton's old apartment over the garage that's empty and I've been planning on renting it out. I could rent it to you until you find another place." Tanner didn't even look at her as he spoke. His head was tipped back so he was looking up, but his eyes were closed.

Zoey didn't know how to respond. Every instinct in her wanted to accept so she could be close to him, but her brain was rebelling. Being close to him was just asking for more rejection. He might be playing the nice guy tonight, but he hadn't always.

"Thank you, but I'm sure I'll find something soon. I have thirty days to figure it out."

Tanner's head tipped down slowly and his amber colored eyes nailed hers in place. He looked speculative and slightly disappointed but he shrugged. "Suit yourself. It's there if you need it. You know where to find me."

Zoey sighed with relief as he let the subject drop and they both focused on an old movie playing on TV. It was for the best, even if her heart and her libido disagreed. She had enough emotional turmoil to face between her mom being back, a new job, and house hunting. No, this was just the way it had to be. Zoey Carson needed to keep her distance from Tanner Keegan. Period.

## CHAPTER THREE

*T*HREE WEEKS LATER...

"I'm sorry, Jan, but for a moment I thought you said that my checking account was overdrawn." Zoey closed her eyes instead of staring at her ceiling, as she spoke with Jan Kostecki at Community Bank.

The indrawn breath was measured, as though Jan was expecting Zoey to blow up, or worse yet cry, and Zoey knew instantly that she had heard her correctly. "Yes, Miss Carson. First thing this morning, a check came in for eleven hundred and eighty dollars and I was unable to clear it for the gentleman because you are overdrawn by thirty-four dollars. With the overdraft charge of twenty dollars, that will make you negative fifty-four dollars."

"Jan, I can do the math, but I can't figure out where the money went. I have over five thousand dollars in there. It's money I've been holding onto from my last set of student loans. I planned to use it to help me get going in this new house." Zoey was trying to hold onto the thin string of calm that she had left. Somehow every penny she had pinched was mysteriously gone. And that gentleman that Jan was talking about was Mr. Finch who was going to be Zoey's new landlord.

"I'm sorry, Miss Carson, but it seems there is some confusion. You had three separate withdraws for fifteen hundred dollars over the last three weeks that used up the bulk of your funds." Jan was speaking, but Zoey was no longer listening. Three weeks was exactly the length of time that her mother had been in town, and in her apartment.

Somehow Eve had managed to steal Zoey's money right out from under her nose, and do it without ever letting on that something was amiss. "Jan, my name is Zoey, not Miss Carson. You've known me my whole life, please don't talk to me like I'm just a random customer. Now, can you tell me how those funds were withdrawn?"

"Oh, well uh, the first was a check cashed at the Merc, and...oh wait, yes all three were cashed there. Three checks in the same amount cashed at the Mercantile's guest service desk, but dear, don't you remember writing them?" Jan sounded perplexed, and Zoey snorted as she let out a sharp laugh.

"No, I certainly do not remember writing them, because I didn't do it. Someone forged those checks, Jan, and I have a pretty good idea who." Zoey rolled over and sat up on the edge of her bed. Her mom hadn't returned home last night, but that wasn't a big shocker. It was most likely that Eve had found someone to shack up with for the night and was too drunk to get herself home.

"Oh my, I'm so sorry, Miss Car—I mean Zoey. If it's fraudulent you need to go see the Sherriff as soon as possible and report it. I doubt the Merc has security cameras, but perhaps they will know more based on the signatures on the checks."

Jan continued to patter on for a few moments about fraud, and the differences in how electronic and paper issues were handled by the bank, but Zoey wasn't listening. She was staring at the bare corner where her mother's suitcase had sat since she arrived. Eve had lit out. As usual, she had come just long enough to take what she wanted and left Zoey to clean up the mess.

"Jan, um, I need to go, but thank you for calling me. I will be in later to talk with Donny and see if I can get a loan. I am supposed to start my new job today, so I need to finish getting ready and get to work. I will call Sherriff Montgomery as soon as possible to make a report."

She waited two full seconds after hanging up with Jan before she was dialing her mother's cell phone number. For just over three weeks, Eve had been living in her home, eating her food, taking forty-five minute showers, and enjoying her hospitality rent free, only to disappear without notice. Zoey couldn't decide if she was more angry about the stolen money, or the lack of a goodbye. Eve's voicemail picked up and she had to force herself to hang up without leaving a message. She wanted to be sure to say everything she needed to in person, not on an answering system.

Zoey managed to put her phone down before her eyes filled with tears, but she fought to keep them in. She couldn't let her mother have that. It was her own fault for allowing a junkie into her home, and giving her free reign amongst her things. So much for her perfect apartment, and all of the plans that had seemed to fall together so smoothly. Mr. Finch had already told her there was competition for the house, that's why she had written the check for the whole security deposit and first month's rent a week ahead of time. He was even going to let her move in over the weekend so she would have more time to clear out her old place before her deadline.

She swallowed hard as she picked up the phone again, and made the quick call to Mr. Finch to explain what had happened. As always he was kind but resolute about the fact he couldn't hold the house for her, he had bills to pay after all. Zoey could feel her dreams drifting away on the fog of cigarette smoke her mother had left behind in her apartment. She was starting her new job at ten a.m. today, and she would officially be homeless in seven days. Not only were the walls crumbling around her, but she could feel the floor of her world caving in too.

It wasn't enough that her dear old mother arrive on her doorstep out of the blue. No, she had to steal everything Zoey had, including her happiness.

Thirty minutes later, Zoey had made a verbal report with the Sherriff's office and agreed to stop by there after work to sign her statement. The deputy on duty was pleasant enough as he explained that she may or may not get the funds back from the bank, and that if they were able to determine there was enough evidence to charge her mother with the crime, they would still have to track her down to arrest her. Unfortunately, it still wouldn't bring back the money she had taken. Zoey knew that every penny was probably long gone or would be within days, and she wouldn't show her face for a very long time if she was smart.

Slowly blending concealer over the red circles of stress that ringed her wide blue eyes, she debated calling Rachel. There was no way that she wanted to move in with the Brooks family, but she really had no other option at this point. Living with a newborn baby, her career successful-newlywed best friend, and her four smoking hot husbands was yet another slap in her face, but at least it wasn't living out of her car. Rachel was still on family medical leave from having Juliet, but now she was juggling taking care of Sawyer after his knee surgery and handling the baby. A houseguest was probably the last thing she needed.

Picking up her phone again as she shook her hair out of the headband that had been keeping it out of her newly made up face, she placed the phone call to Rachel.

"Hey, Zoey! What's up?"

Rachel's voice triggered the monsoon of tears that she had been fighting, and before she could do anything to stop it, she was sobbing out the whole shitty story. She knew that no matter what, her best friend wouldn't judge her for her mother's bad behavior. If anyone understood what it was like to have a parent hurt them, it was Rachel.

"That fucking bitch! Who does she think she is? When I get my hands on her—"

Zoey barked out a laugh, "Good luck with that, she's long gone. I'm not sure if she took her stuff out yesterday while I was gone, or if she snuck in last night and got it, but she packed up and bolted."

"Sweet Jesus. Is there no decency in her at all? I'm so sorry, Zoey. I can't even imagine...what are you going to do?"

"I talked to the Sherriff's office, and they weren't very optimistic about me getting my money back. Even if I do, it will be awhile. Who knows where she is by now. I have seven days to figure out where I'm going to live, pack up my whole apartment, and move. Plus, I'm starting my new job in an hour, and now I have to do my makeup again. Goddamn her!"

"Oh no! The eviction! Oh shit, Zoey, I completely forgot you were on a time crunch!"

"Yeah, just another thing to add to the growing shit pile. Rach, I know it's a lot to ask, but can I take you up on your offer of the guest room for a couple of weeks?" Zoey held her breath when Rachel hesitated. She felt the room start to spin and she sank to the floor of her bathroom with her eyes clenched shut.

"Zoey, my mom just got here yesterday and she's in the guest room. She came down for a couple of weeks to help me take care of Jules while Sawyer is down from his surgery. I'm so sorry, if I had known…"

Zoey knew Rachel hadn't planned it on purpose, but it sucked anyways. Rachel was Zoey's plan B, and now that Plan A and Plan B were gone, she was royally screwed.

"That's it then, I'll be crashing in my car for a little bit. I might need to borrow your driveway to park in. I mean, I can't imagine the school board will like it much if I'm parked in the parking lot every night, and I have no idea what kind of office I will have, so I can't plan on sleeping there—"

"Stop it, Zoey! Right now!" Rachel broke through the panic that was growing in her chest, and Zoey inhaled deeply trying to calm her racing heart. "There is another option you know? I know it's not ideal, but what if you rent Tanner's apartment just for a couple of weeks and if you want to move here when Mom leaves, the offer is still open."

Like a flash in her brain she could see Tanner sprawled out in the Brooks family living room asking her if she wanted to rent Dalton's old apartment over the garage. Beautiful, dark, sexy Tanner. Could she live under the same roof with him and not make a fool out of herself? He had been kind enough to offer, and she was really desperate, but it seemed like the worst possible scenario for her heart.

"I don't know."

"Zoey, you don't have a choice. You can't live in your car and start a respectable career."

Rachel was right, and at that moment Zoey hated her for it. Her brain was at war with her heart and as always logic won out. "I'll call him when I get a break, but Rachel, it's only until your mom leaves, okay?"

"You got it. The moment mom heads back to Oklahoma I'll have the guys help move you in. Now, clean yourself up, and get your ass to your new job! You are going to rock it and those kids will love you."

Her enthusiasm made Zoey smile for the first time all morning, and she forced herself to her feet after saying her goodbyes. Rachel was right. She was starting the road to the rest of her life today one way or another, and this was just a little hurdle she had to cross before it smoothed out again.

Two or three weeks in Dalton's old apartment wouldn't kill her, and besides, Tanner was a rancher. He was in the saddle from sunup to sundown, so really as long as she made sure she was tucked safely behind closed doors before sunset, she wouldn't even have to deal with him. It would all work out perfectly in the end. She was going to make sure of it.

---

Tanner was just stepping onto the front porch of the house when the sound of a car coming down his drive caught his attention. He turned and rested one hip against the porch railing as Zoey Carson parked and threw open her car door. The melodic sounds of Kenny Chesney singing about addiction in his song "Demons" drifted on the breeze. A pang of hurt zipped through his heart for Zoey and the heartache he figured her mother's problems had brought into her life. He didn't know the details, but he did understand how hard the battle with addiction could be.

He waited patiently as she climbed out of her twenty-year-old car, and took a few measured steps toward him. Her eyes darted around for a few seconds without meeting his, and he bit his tongue to keep from smiling. It was good to know that he kept her as off balance as she did him.

"Hi, Tanner."

"Well. Well. Well. What brings you all the way out to the Triple T?"

She cleared her throat, and took a deep breath. Her knuckles were white where she gripped her tiny purse at her hip, and she shoved her other hand into her hair in a nervous gesture. "Actually, um, do you mind if we go inside? It's awfully hot out here."

Tanner stepped back and held his arm out gallantly for her to lead the way. As she brushed past him, her long black hair swished against his arm and sent a spiral of need straight to his groin. It was like silk against his skin, and he could just imagine what it would feel like draped over his chest as she rode him to a screaming orgasm.

Her round hips swayed as she stepped up inside the front door, and he saw her shoulders droop slightly when the chill of the air-conditioned house hit her. She moved over to the sofa and perched her lush ass daintily on the edge of the tufted suede with that miniature purse in her lap.

Tanner turned and dropped his hat on the table next to the door before bending to tug his boots off with his back to her. For a moment he thought he might cut his own cock in half when he bent over, but by the time he was in his socks and comfortable, he felt under control again. Until he turned around and caught Zoey's eyes on his backside. Instantly he was hard as stone again. This time he spread his thighs and narrowed his eyes on her.

Zoey's gaze landed on the bulge beneath his zipper for just a breath in time before she blushed and turned away. *So that was the way of it.* Well good, at least this time she wasn't half drunk and begging him to take her to bed.

A picture of her spread out on his bed with her dark hair on his crisp white pillow and her pretty pink lips open and gasping for air hit him hard, and he grunted, startling her. "Did you need something, Zoey, or did you just come here to sit on my sofa in silence?"

Her jaw clenched in irritation but she seemed resolved to whatever she had to say. "I need a favor, Tanner."

Tanner felt his eyebrow lift and he let his eyes run over her stiffened spine and knees clenched tightly together. This might get more interesting after all.

"Okay, is this a whiskey kind of favor or a beer kind of favor?" He turned and moved toward the kitchen that opened up on the other side of the living room.

"What?"

"Just trying to determine how strong of a beverage I'm going to need for this chat. What's the favor?"

"I need to know if I can stay with you for a couple of weeks. I mean, in Dalton's apartment. Can I rent it for a couple of weeks?" She held her breath when she was nervous, and there went her hand running through her hair again. When she let loose, it fell in a gentle wavy pattern that looked downright sexy on her.

"Why?" Tanner tugged the fridge open and pulled out a bottle of beer, holding up with a questioning look to Zoey. When she shook her head no, he grabbed her a bottle of water and moved back into the living room.

"If you recall my place was bought by the new developer who moved to town, and I only had thirty days to move. Unfortunately, some things have happened and the house that I put a deposit on…well it fell through. Rachel would take me in, but her mom is staying with her for a couple of weeks while Sawyer recovers from his surgery, so it leaves me without a place to stay."

Tanner took a seat on the sofa next to her, even though he knew he should probably keep his distance. She looked so nervous he reached out and patted her arm. "Come on, it didn't hurt that much to ask me, did it?"

Her lips curled up in a small smile, "You would be surprised."

"Normally, it would be no big deal for you to use the apartment, but I just got word that Dalton will be home this weekend."

Her gorgeous blue eyes widened and she looked as stunned as Tanner had felt when he picked up the phone the evening before. Dalton hadn't been home since their Dad's heart attack, and Tanner had begun to believe the next time he would see his younger brother would be for a funeral.

"Dalton? But, I thought he was in Africa doing charity work with Borders for Doctors?" Zoey's hands twisted the cap on the bottle of water as though tightening it would help hold her spine straight while she asked for his help.

"Doctors without Borders. Yeah, he has been. For nearly a decade. However, the MSF organization is pulling out of Somalia. It has something to do with the safety of the workers. He called yesterday and asked me to pick him up at the airport Friday. Shocked the shit out of me too."

"So he's just going to move back here and live in Stone River after all this time?"

He shrugged and took a drink of his beer. He had been asking himself the same questions and still hadn't come up with any answers. There was a small clinic in Stone River, but the closest hospital was in Austin. It didn't make sense for a qualified doctor to settle in a small town unless he was opening his own practice, and Dalton had never wanted a private practice before.

"I don't know. We didn't have much time to discuss his plans. I guess I will find out when he gets here."

For several moments they sat in silence as Zoey chewed on the new information. Tanner waited her out because he wasn't sure she would accept the alternative anyways. When her chin quivered and her blue eyes filled with tears, his heart lurched in his chest and he inhaled sharply like he had been sucker punched.

She started to stand up, and pull her purse strap over her shoulder, "Okay, well thanks anyways."

Unable to control his own hand he reached out to grab her wrist. "Wait a second. I didn't say no."

Zoey looked down at his fingers wrapped around her tiny wrist. It felt as thin as a twig under his callused skin, and he had the distinct urge to wrap her up and protect her.

Clearing his throat, he continued, "I just said you can't stay in the apartment. This house has another unoccupied bedroom, and you're welcome to use it. Free of rent."

Her pretty face went pale and then pink spots appeared on her cheeks. "Stay here, in the main house, with you?"

"I'm not going to molest you, Jesus. What kind of a man do you think I am?" Tanner dropped her wrist and surged to his feet, stomping to the front door. "You know what, never mind. I wouldn't want someone here who is scared of me anyways."

"No! I'm not scared of you! I just—look, the truth is, I'm kind of having a really shitty day. My mom took off sometime last night with all of my money and my groceries, and I started my new job today, only to find out that I'm a glorified secretary for the real school counselor. I get to bring her coffee and pick up her dry cleaning, all the while filing and typing up her letters. I only have seven days to figure out where to live or I will be living in my car, and my best friend has the perfect life with her perfect family and no room to help me out right now. I need the place to stay, and before I have a nervous breakdown let me say, yes. I will gladly accept it with the free rent, as long as you let me do something to help out around here."

Tanner stood back watching her fall to pieces and then pick herself right back up again. She was absolutely amazing. Not only had her mother betrayed her and stolen from her, but she had left her to clean up the shambles that were left behind. Somehow, Zoey was managing to hold herself together when Tanner wasn't sure he would have been able to do the same. For being so young, she certainly had a strong backbone. Another clue that she was not the submissive woman he needed for his lifemate.

He knew that he should probably ask her about her mother, but the strain on her face had him backing off, and instead he gave her a smile to break the tension. "Are you any good at mucking stalls?"

She snorted out a laugh in an unladylike way, and he chuckled. "No, and I'm not an expert at riding a horse either, but you know that I can cook, and I can clean. You're a bachelor, so surely that means something to you?"

He groaned, "Sweet Jesus, if you'll cook for me you can live here forever."

Realizing what he said, he grimaced, but Zoey only smiled brighter. "It's only for a few weeks. I'll either find another place, or move in with Rachel as soon as her mom leaves. Thank you, Tanner!"

He forced himself to shrug nonchalantly. "Do you need a hand moving? Like I said, Dalton will be back sometime Friday night. I'm sure we can come over to your place to help move boxes Saturday."

She looked surprised but pleased, and he felt a funny warmth in his chest at her happiness. "That would be amazing! I'm going to have to cook my ass off to repay you."

"That's not necessary, just a home cooked dinner every now and then will suffice." She reached out and gave him a quick hug, her breasts pressing against his ribcage, and her hair brushing his chin. His cock was instantly trying to burst out of his jeans, and he barely resisted wrapping his arms around her and drawing her closer. What would it be like to reach around and grab that perfect ass, pulling her off her feet so she had to wrap her legs around his hips...a rush of heat shot from his brain to his balls and he cleared his throat again, stepping back. She released him, and her teary eyes looked up at him as if he had just rescued her from a nightmarish dragon.

"Well I better get home. I have to be up early for work, and I haven't packed yet. Thank you again, Tanner. I don't know what I would have done...well, just thank you."

"You're welcome, Zoey. That's what friends are for." He shifted his stance, trying to give his throbbing cock room in his jeans, and held the front door open as she stepped into the doorway. She paused and glanced back.

"Friends? Is that what we are?"

"Well I hope so, it would be mighty awkward to have an enemy living in my own house."

He relished her husky laughter as she made her way to her car. There was a bounce in her steps that hadn't been there before, and he was ridiculously pleased to have helped her obtain it.

Once she had disappeared down the road, Tanner realized what he had just agreed to. The one woman who seemed to be his Kryptonite was not only going to be sharing his house but, would also be sleeping on the other side of a thin wall, and sharing his bathroom. Yeah, sure, there was no way this could go wrong.

He slammed the door shut, and immediately popped the buttons on his jeans open allowing his cock to jut out. The dark purple head stared back at him with a pearly drop oozing out of it. Leaning his back against the door, he fisted it while the smell of Zoey hung heavy in the air, and he could still feel her full breasts against his body.

It took only a half dozen strokes before he filled his own fist with cum, and let out a loud groan that echoed through the empty house. He had no doubt it would be the first of many lonely encounters over the next month or so.

If he'd had a choice, he would have pushed her to her knees and asked her to thank him in a more intimate way, but it would have started an avalanche of problems that Tanner didn't need right now. Instead, he would most likely spend the next couple of weeks walking and working with a hard-on from hell.

Only a fool would agree to live with a woman who boiled his blood, and was completely and utterly off limits to him. A quick glance in the hallway mirror as he headed for the bathroom to clean up proved the fool was present and accounted for and was asking for trouble.

## CHAPTER FOUR

DALTON KEEGAN WAS HOME. He was on US soil. Good old Texas dirt. It felt wonderful and terrible all at once.

The first time he walked through the Austin-Bergstrom Airport he believed he was leaving Texas behind for good. He was on his way to medical school, and had no intention of coming back, even though he had made promises to his parents to visit every holiday he could. He held his ground for four years, only breaking down and visiting the summer after graduation. The look on his mother's face when he announced his plans to leave for Africa was a unique juxtaposition of pride and disappointment. He knew she wanted him to stay close, but at the time he couldn't handle the open floodgates to his memories that living in Texas would mean.

One emergency visit back home was all he allowed himself in the nearly ten years he had been overseas. But after seeing that pops was recovered from his heart attack, and that his mother was making plans to retire in Arizona, Dalton's heart was in pieces, and he was ready to escape again at any cost. He left with a lighter heart because with his parents in Arizona, he would have the ability to visit them there and never again have to face his past in the Lone Star state.

Apparently, life had other plans for him. Just a mere two weeks ago they had gotten word at the camp in Mogadishu, Somalia, the organization was pulling all personnel out of the country. The violence had been escalating and the government factors weren't being as helpful in discouraging the attacks on volunteer doctors and nurses. Dalton had seen a handful of volunteers killed in the years he had been over there, but it held no comparison to the thousands who died every year from malnutrition and disease because they couldn't get help in time.

He was angry to be pulled out, but he had no say in the matter. He wasn't ready to sign onto another position in another country, and his parents lived in a retirement community in Arizona. There was no extra room for him to live there, so here he was back in small town Texas for the time being.

Being back in Stone River meant facing the demons he had been running from for the last two decades, and he wasn't exactly sure yet how to accomplish that. Running into Walt or Minnie White would be his worst nightmare, and yet in a small town like Stone River, it was going to be impossible to avoid them.

"Professor!"

The sound of his older brother's voice echoed through the doorway of the airport terminal, and Dalton couldn't stop the grin that spread across his face. Even facing his worst fears wasn't going to stop him from enjoying the time with his brother. He had missed the stupid nicknames, jokes, and even the backbreaking work that came with being home on the Triple T.

Dalton made a beeline for Tanner, whose broad cowboy build drew the eyes of the female population anywhere he went. Tanner never even noticed the dozens of sighs from women as he ambled through a public place because it was normal for him. His bearing was that of a proud Army general, and Dalton knew from experience that Tanner ran the ranch with the same efficiency.

Dropping his carry-on to the floor, he wrapped his brother in a masculine embrace of backslapping, chest pounding Alpha male greeting. "Skipper! Damn it's good to see you!"

"You too, man," Tanner responded with a chuckle. They had quirky nicknames for each other out of love, or at least it was love on Dalton's part. Years ago, watching Gilligan's Island had been the highlight of their after school ritual. Tanner was Skipper because he was supposed to be in charge, but his brothers made sure his ego never got too big. Dalton was always a Straight A Honor Roll student, so he was Professor, and that left Clint with the nickname Gilligan. Poor kid had started out as gangly and awkward as possible. It wasn't until he hit fourteen when he finally filled out. After that, the girls went gaga for him. It was still weird to Dalton that Clint was in Hollywood working as an actor.

"Did you check bags?"

"Nah, I shipped my stuff back. It should be here in a couple of days. Just me and my pack." The two brothers turned and headed across the airport. Dalton caught more than a few double takes as they moved through the crowd. People parted easily in front of the two big men, but it didn't stop Dalton from feeling a little claustrophobic in the mass of bodies.

Their size was the first thing most people noticed when they were together. At six foot tall, they weren't giants, but thanks to their parents great gene mash up, they were both broadly built and muscular. To help pay for medical school, Dalton had even posed for a few modeling companies at one point. His blonde hair and blue eyes stood out in sharp contrast to Tanner's darker coloring and amber colored eyes, but they shared similar features in their oval faces, angular jaws, and long narrow noses. If Clint stood with them, the similarities in the three men were even more obvious. Clint had his mother and Tanner's darker coloring, and toffee brown eyes. They were ringed with thick eyelashes that drove the ladies crazy. His dimpled chin was identical to Dalton's, and they all three shared the same thick eyebrows and strong brow line. Yep, they were three brothers who looked alike, but couldn't have been more different from each other.

They stepped out into the stifling Texas heat and Dalton threw his head back, inhaling deeply. "Ahh, it even smells different here."

Tanner laughed, "You're probably smelling the horse shit on my boots. I came directly from working all day long."

"Can't say I've missed mucking stalls, but I can't wait to get back in a saddle." Dalton tossed his backpack in the back end of Tanner's old pickup truck and climbed up onto the cracked vinyl seat.

Country music blared out of the speakers when Tanner turned the key, and Dalton couldn't resist tapping his tennis shoe to the chorus about "Boys Round Here." He hadn't been able to listen to much American music unless it was already programmed onto his iPod. He couldn't wait to spend a day searching all of the newest hits to supplement his small selection.

"So how was Africa?"

"Hot, dirty, and fantastic. I'm going to miss it."

"Any word on whether or not the program will be able to reopen?"

Dalton shook his head, and sighed. "No, and until they can work something out with the government, I don't see it happening. Could be after twenty years, MSF will just have to stay out of Somalia."

"It's a damn shame when people are attacking volunteers who are only there to help save lives and feed them," Tanner said, and Dalton nodded his agreement.

"It's a warzone. Anything goes in a warzone. There's been so much conflict that most of the time no one is even sure who is on whose side. We were there to help everyone. Didn't matter which side they were on, or what they had done in the past or might do in the future. The only thing that mattered was they needed help."

Tanner snorted, "So you helped fix up the guys who were more than likely going to turn around and shoot you the first chance they had?"

Dalton shook his head, "No it's not like that. I mean, sure, there is a chance of it, but for the most part, we are passing out food to people who are starving and treating them for diseases they've contracted because they don't have the right stuff available. Anyways, I don't want to talk about work. Tell me about Stone River? What's changed at the Triple T?"

"Not much, man. I'm still working with the sun and falling into bed half dead at night. I just started working with Brooks Pastures to coordinate our breeding programs."

"What?" Dalton stared at Tanner in shock. For decades the Triple T and Brooks Pastures had been in competition with each other. The idea the two families might work together had honestly never occurred to him.

"Yeah, Parker and Rogan have one hell of a stallion over there, and if I can get a few foals with some of our mares, well, I think it will serve us all well." Tanner glanced at Dalton's stunned face and grimaced. "Times have changed Professor. We can't all avoid what's happening around us by packing up and moving. I have to adjust our system or risk going under."

Dalton hissed out a breath of air he hadn't realized he was holding, "Shit, I'm sorry. You just surprised me. Are things that bad in Stone River?"

"Not bad so much as the bills are tight. We have had three straight years of drought. The Carrion River is way down, and the cost of water has gone up, so bringing more in isn't an option. I have to find a way to keep us afloat without the crops."

It was quiet between the two brothers for a few moments as Dalton pondered Tanner's response. He was right of course. Changes had to be made in order to protect the ranch, and after almost fifteen years out of the ranching business, Dalton was the last person with a right to judge his older brother for his business decisions.

"Good for you."

Tanner barked out a surprised laugh.

"I mean it, Skipper. That ranch is your heart and soul, and I admire you for doing whatever it takes to save it. If the Brooks boys are the way to do that, then I'm all for it."

"Glad to hear it, because you're going to have to help me explain it to pops when he comes to visit at Christmas. I haven't told him yet."

"Oh shit! Nope, you're on your own with that, man. Besides, I'm not sure yet where I'll be at Christmas time. I have a couple of months to figure it out."

Tanner frowned, "If it means anything to you, it would make mama really happy if you would stick around for it. There are jobs in Austin, or old Doc Plass might be looking to retire? You have a home at the ranch, so you don't have to leave if you don't want to."

Dalton turned his head to look out the window of the truck at the passing scenery. Now that they were on the highway there was only fields, cows, and the occasional scrub brush to look at, but he wasn't going to let Tanner see the tears in his eyes. He wanted to be able to say yes. If only he had that option.

"We'll see. I'm not sure Stone River can ever be my home again, Tanner. It wouldn't be fair to Minnie and Walt."

"Are you kidding? You're still holding on to that? Walt and Minnie have grieved and moved on, Dalton. If they've managed to let it go, why can't you?"

"Because they didn't kill anyone, Tanner. I did. I will never be able to forgive myself, and they shouldn't have to see their son's murderer every day for the rest of their lives."

"Dalton—"

"No! I don't want to have this conversation right now. I just got my feet back on US soil and I want to use this time to rest. Do me a favor and let me know when we hit Stone River. I'm going to take a little cat nap." Dalton promptly shut his eyes and ignored Tanner's cursed mutterings under his breath. His brother was wrong. There was no way Walt and Minnie would ever move on and forgive him for Ben's death. As well they shouldn't. Forcing the whole thing from his mind, Dalton let his body relax and quickly slipped into sleep with the rocking of the truck.

---

Tanner's battered red truck pulled up in front of Zoey's place at ten o'clock on the nose Saturday morning. Like any good weirdo, Zoey was watching for it from her apartment window. When the two broad-shouldered men climbed out, she could just barely hear their laughter through the thin glass, and a ripple of desire shot through her. Tanner's cowboy hat was missing, leaving his buzzed head bare to her view, and when paired up with Dalton's lighter sandy blonde hair they almost looked like a cowboy version of Good versus Evil. She wasn't sure which option she wanted to taste first, the good or the evil, but at this moment neither was actually a choice.

Hurrying across the large room, she glanced around at the empty corners. She really didn't have a whole lot that was hers. The sofa and chair along with most of the living room contents belonged to the landlord, as did the bed and dresser. That left her with just a stack of about twelve moving boxes, her bike, her television, and the cedar chest that she and Rachel had found at a flea market when they were seventeen. They had spent a whole month lovingly restoring the piece and it was Zoey's most prized possession.

When the doorbell rang, Zoey plastered a smile on and swung it open. She was anticipating the blast of sex appeal from Tanner, but the electricity nearly singed her when her eyes met Dalton's.

"Zoey Carson. Wow! I haven't seen you since you were in pigtails," Dalton said. His slightly shell-shocked appearance soothed her ego a little and she sighed.

"Ah yes, Dalton the demi-God who broke dozens of teenage hearts in Stone River when he left for medical school!" She threw back dramatically. His laughter was warm and he stepped forward wrapping her in a hug.

"Damn it's good to see you too, woman. You grew up good!" Dalton's hand rested on her hip with his arm holding her close, in an affectionate sort of way, as he looked her over. She returned the favor taking in his golden locks, dimpled chin, and midnight blue eyes. That combo alone would make for a teenage wet dream, but when settled over the top of a six foot tall perfectly sculpted specimen of man meat, it was nuclear.

"I'm not the only one. Age has done you well, Mr. Keegan." She threw a glance at Tanner, surprised to find him glaring at the pair of them. "Morning, Tanner, is everything alright?"

"It's fine. If you two are done drooling on each other, I would like to get a move on loading this stuff up. Unlike you two, I have chores to do when we get back." He sounded gruff, but Zoey saw his eyes roam over her semi-empty place and soften when he realized what a small pile of belongings there was to move. "Did you get everything packed, Zoey?"

"Yep, this is it. Once we have it all loaded I just need to drop the key off to Mrs. Flannigan downstairs. Mr. Langley is going to be by tomorrow to collect all of the keys from her. She has a moving company coming to help move her out today." She was still standing in the curve of Dalton's arm, but sensing that it was making Tanner tense she took a step away from his younger brother and slid her hands into her back pockets. "Thank you both for helping me out. I'm sure Rogan, Parker, and Hudson would have, but with Sawyer down and the new baby—"

"New baby? What new baby?" Dalton asked, looking confused.

"The Brooks brothers married Rachel Morgan. You remember Rachel, she and I are best friends. The five of them got married almost a year ago now, and they just had a little girl named Juliet."

"Fuck me! You have got to be kidding. Parker Brooks got someone to marry him? And he has a kid? Wait, did you just say all four of them are married to her? How the hell does that work?"

Tanner and Zoey shared a look and a laugh, "Oddly enough, brother, it seems to work for them. She married Rogan legally, but they are all well and truly married to her."

"And the town didn't burn her at the stake for bewitching the four of them?" Dalton joked, and Zoey started giggling harder.

"Nope, in fact they seem to have embraced and accepted their family pretty easily. It's unusual, but as long as they aren't hurting anyone, they are allowed to love whoever they want."

"Alright, you can catch up on all of the gossip at home. I'm sure Zoey will be glad to fill you in. Let's get moving." Tanner picked up the closest box and passed it to Dalton's waiting arms.

"You got it boss," Dalton said with a sharp nod to Tanner and a wink at Zoey before he spun on his heel and marched out of the apartment.

"I see your brother is still an enormous flirt," Zoey said, picking up a smaller box and following behind Tanner as he carried two boxes at once.

Tanner snorted, "Are you surprised? Dalton's flirting was legendary. There's no way Africa could change him that much."

Zoey dropped the subject as they stepped out into the sunshine and Dalton relieved her of her armful. Tanner might think Dalton had all of the flirting skills, but he wasn't giving himself enough credit. He had been doing a number on her body ever since she was thirteen and she spotted him and Lindsay Self making out in the back of Dottie's ice cream shop. How she was going to survive even a couple of weeks in the same house as these two was anyone's guess.

The scent of food drifted on the air as Dalton stepped into the living room, and his stomach growled. How long had it been since he had eaten a home cooked dinner?

Watching from the end of the hallway, he looked Zoey over. She had certainly grown into a stunning woman. Her curvy body was on the shorter side, but she far made up for it with her big personality. She was sexy as hell, and his cock took note as her long black hair swung down her back with her movements. Her back was to him as she worked at the stove, and if he wanted a better look at her perfectly round ass, he would have to move closer.

"Something smells delicious," he said as he walked across the living room. Her head came up and she turned those enormous blue eyes on him with a million dollar smile.

"Tanner doesn't keep the kitchen very well stocked, so I'm making do tonight. I found a beef pot roast in the freezer and I made up some egg noodles. There's corn bread in the oven, would you mind setting the table?"

Dalton smiled back at the easy way Zoey made herself at home. The girl hadn't even had time to unpack her stuff, and yet she was scrambling around the kitchen making noodles from scratch. She was a gem. "You got it, pretty lady, and believe me, I'm not a picky eater. If you knew some of the things I've eaten during the last ten years..." He shivered and shook his head making her laugh. The husky tinkle of her giggle went straight to his nuts and the moment her back was to him, he adjusted himself.

It had been months since he'd had sex, and his dick was as hard as a wooden fence post just being close to a gorgeous woman. Her scent was a blend of almond and honey and he wanted to lick her skin to see if she tasted that way too.

"So how does it feel to be back in the US?"

"Weird. It's just as hot here, but it's a lot cleaner. I miss the work, and I miss the people, but I'm beginning to wonder if the world is trying to tell me that I needed to move on." Dalton had the table set pretty quickly, and he moved back to the kitchen to watch Zoey again.

"You've been gone a long time. Give yourself a few days to adjust," she responded easily as she bent over to pull the bread from the oven.

A groan slipped from his throat at the sight of her perfectly heart shaped ass, and she stood quickly. He could see her cheeks turning red and he sighed. "I'm sorry, Zoey. I'm not trying to make you uncomfortable. You have to know how beautiful you are, and I've been out of the dating scene for a long time. Forgive me."

She waved a hand at him, "There's nothing to forgive. Just forget it. Can you let Tanner know that dinner's ready?"

"You just did." Tanner appeared from the direction of the living room and by the glare he was giving Dalton, he had heard their conversation. "Smells fantastic, Zoey. Anything I can do?"

"No thanks Tanner, just take a seat at the table. I'll bring it over in just a second." She bustled around collecting various things and bringing them to the dining table as Dalton and Tanner both took their seats. It felt too good to have her there, serving them dinner at their mothers table, and Dalton had to check himself.

He had barely been back and he was already considering making a play for a woman that his brother clearly had his hat set for already. What kind of an idiot was he? He forced his thoughts back to dinner and making polite conversation, trying hard to forget the lovely bit of female who sat across from him. Did she know she made a sexy O with her full lips when she blew on her spoon of noodles? Would she look that hot with his cock in her mouth?

A flash of heat shot down his spine and his cock throbbed in his jeans. Fidgeting to find a comfortable seat, Dalton turned to Tanner instead. "Heard anything out of Clint?"

"No, and I didn't really expect to."

"But he turned thirty last week, I would have thought…" Dalton's voice trailed off and he looked back to his bowl.

"Thought what? That he would actually stick to his word and come back to the ranch?" Tanner snapped. "Yeah sure, and I'll grow a tail and start braying like a donkey too. Clint won't do anything he doesn't want to."

Zoey stared at the two of them, and a small worry line creased her brow. "I'm missing something."

"Our baby brother made a promise to our mother that if he didn't have a great acting career by the time he was thirty he would come back to the ranch," Tanner said with a snort. "Other than a few commercials, the last I heard he was working for a lawn care service in L.A. Sorry, Professor, but I highly doubt he follows through on that promise."

Dalton sighed with frustration. This was how it worked between them. Tanner was cynical, Clint was flighty, and Dalton played mediator. "I sent him an email to let him know I was coming home, maybe he will get in touch and at least let us know he's okay."

"You guys don't keep in touch?" Zoey's question wasn't so much odd as uncomfortable. Dalton had never liked the fact that he had drifted so far away from his brothers, and having her point it out made him feel like an ass.

"Not really. We've all been busy."

She took a sip of water and shrugged. "I always wanted siblings when I was a kid. Rachel is pretty much my sister, and until she had Juliet and got busier, we talked every other day. I can't imagine not making time for your brothers."

"Do you talk to your mother every day?" Tanner asked softly and Dalton frowned when Zoey's face went pale. There was more to that question, and his protective instinct jumped to the surface when she fumbled with her spoon.

"Shut up, Tanner. She was just making an observation, and she's right. Even if you don't like it." Dalton turned back to Zoey with a small smile, "Dinner is wonderful, pretty lady, thank you for taking the time to cook it for us. Tanner and I will clean up to show you how appreciative we are."

She smiled but it was still shaky, "You're welcome. I love cooking, but I haven't had much of a chance to do it with just me to cook for. Any favorites I should add to the menu?"

He brightened at her question, "Do you know how to make fried chicken?"

She rolled her eyes laughing, "I'm from Texas. Of course I know how to make fried chicken."

"Marry me," he said, playfully sighing and grabbing her hand from across the table. When she laughed and shook her head, warmth filled his chest. He was looking forward to hearing that sound from her more often.

"I can't marry you, you don't have a job."

Dalton reached out and tweaked her nose with his fingertip, "Well I'm calling dibs on it when you change your mind. As long as you cook for me, I will promise you all of the hot sex you want. Any time, any place."

Zoey's cheeks turned pink and she laughed, but Dalton could tell she was turned on. Her lush pink lips parted and her eyes sparkled with a fire that he hadn't noticed before. It hinted at a deep well of passion that Dalton's cock absolutely wanted the chance to explore.

*Hmmm...coming home might not have been such a bad thing.* Tanner intervened and changed the subject. No amount of superficial chat altered the course of his fantasies though, and by the end of the evening, Dalton hurried up to his apartment with the sole intention of alleviating the hard-on that was mashed against his zipper.

Living with Zoey Carson might prove to be his undoing.

---

From the kitchen sink, Tanner watched as Zoey settled onto the sofa, tucking her sexy feet under her. She always seemed to be hiding her feet for some reason and it made him want to laugh. Laughing was not going to help the throbbing erection in his jeans though. He wanted to strangle Dalton for all of his flirting and teasing throughout dinner.

Every time he mentioned sex and Zoey in the same breath the temperature of the room seemed to shoot up, and Tanner's jeans got tighter. It didn't help that Zoey seemed interested. Her grapefruit sized tits seemed to lift up and reach out for attention with their hard nipples.

He couldn't resist mulling over what color the tempting tips would be. A lush pink like her lips, or more of a dusky rose color or maybe a soft brown to match her honey sweet scent?

A plate dropped from his hands, shattering in the sink and taking a tiny chunk of his thumb with it.

"Fucking hell!" Before he could move, Zoey was at his side and reaching for his hand. He snatched it back, earning a hard glare from her gorgeous blue eyes.

"Oh stop it. It's just a little cut. Come on, let's go get you cleaned up, and then we can clear away the glass." Her small hand grabbed his forearm and tugged him along behind her until they reached the hallway bathroom.

"What is it about men and injuries? Do they think just because we're women we can't see them bleed?" She crouched down wading through the miscellaneous medical supplies in the cabinet under the sink and before he knew it, she was gently cleaning his injury. Her sexy lips pursed as she blew on the stinging flesh before wrapping it with gauze. "Well, thankfully you won't need stitches. The cut is probably too wide to stitch shut anyways. You should be more careful."

Tanner felt the blow to his pride and he huffed, "The plate slipped out of my hand. It's not like it attacked me."

"Maybe not, but the next injury could be worse." She bent over in the tiny space to put the supplies back, and Tanner sucked in a breath. They were in a small room and she was in front of him, bent practically in half so her heart shaped ass was in a direct line with his aching cock.

"At this rate I'll need stitches in my cock," he grumbled. Zoey stood up so fast she swayed on her feet, and the shock on her face made his blood run cold. He hadn't meant to say that out loud, damn it.

"What?" she whispered, and he felt a flush of embarrassment rise in his cheeks.

"Nothing. I was just commenting about what time it was. I still need to do a few things in the barn after I clean up that glass." Tanner spun on his heel and stomped down the hallway, eager to put some space between them.

Zoey didn't seem to feel the same way as she followed him closely and grabbed his arm when he reached for the broken dish. "No, you go take care of whatever you still need to, I'll clean this up."

"I said I would do the dishes, and I meant it. It was just an accident and a little cut."

"Yes, but you need to let it heal. Sticking it back in that water isn't the way to do that. Besides, I could use a little quiet time to think. You two gave me a lot to think about tonight. Go on out and get your chores done. There are only a couple of dishes left anyways."

She was so damn amenable. Why couldn't she be the bitchy woman he's avoided for the last few years? The one that seemed to loathe him with a never ending well of angry passion.

"Fine, whatever."

He was marching his way out to the barn before he could even think through what she had said. What had they given her to think about, other than sex? His gut tightened. This was turning into a mistake of epic proportions. His dream woman was going to be sleeping in a bed not fifteen feet away from his own king size bed, and now he knew for a fact his younger brother wanted to sleep with her too. What would he do if the two of them hooked up?

Fuck that.

There was no way in hell he was going to let Dalton flirt his way into Zoey's pants. Zoey Carson was off limits, and tomorrow morning he would make that fact crystal clear to Dalton because if he didn't…well… living with Zoey might just be his undoing.

## CHAPTER FIVE

Zoey spent Sunday making herself at home on the Triple T. The house was comfortable, and the kitchen well stocked with every utensil imaginable. She had even found a second freezer full of meat in the laundry room, but there was barely a scrap to be found in the cupboards.

She was making a list of groceries she needed to get, when Dalton came in from outside. His cheeks were flushed red and his blonde hair was windblown. Wearing snug wranglers and borrowed boots, he had slipped back into the Texas cowboy role with ease, and her libido took notice.

"Whew! Fall is on the air today I think," he said as he ran his long fingers through his shaggy locks. "Smells good in here, what are you making?"

"Cinnamon bread to go with the chili for dinner tonight. Is it cold outside?" Zoey tapped the pen against her lips before realizing his eyes were zeroed in on the phallic item against her mouth. She frowned and dropped the pen to her lap.

"No it's not cold, but the wind is strong today. Whatcha doing?" He plopped down next to her, snatching the paper from her lap and throwing one arm behind her across the back of the sofa.

"Hey! I'm making a grocery list. Tanner apparently only eats meat, so there is barely anything in the kitchen to cook with. I found the cinnamon all the way in the back of the top cabinet and it had never even been opened." She tugged the list out of his hands, and smoothed it out before applying her pen to it again. "Is there anything you can think of that I should add to the list? Anything you need?"

Dalton brushed a piece of her long hair back over her ear with a small smile on his face. "At this moment, nothing I need or want can go on that list."

Zoey's stomach clenched her panties grew damp at the subtle hint. He was way too close for comfort with his big body pressing against her side. The blended scent of man and the outdoors filled her nose, making her mouth water. Her hand was shaking a little as she capped the pen and started to stand.

Dalton grabbed the belt loop on the back of her jeans, surprising her and throwing her off balance so she tumbled down on to his lap. "Whoa!"

"Easy now, I just didn't want you to run away from me. You act like you're scared of me, Zoey love, and I would hate for you to be scared of me." He looked down at her with a pair of the sexiest blue bedroom eyes Zoey had ever seen and she shivered.

"I'm not scared of you, but this is inappropriate."

He looked taken aback, and his eyebrow lifted in question, "Why? You're a gorgeous woman and I'm a lonely man. We're both single, so what's the big deal?"

"The big deal is that Zoey is here under my roof and my protection. So you will not be hitting on her or making her uncomfortable, Dalton Keegan." Tanner's voice was hard and cold, and Zoey let out a small 'eep' of surprise before scrambling off Dalton's lap and across the room so she stood an equal distance from the two men.

Tanner filled the doorway to the living room, tapping his heavy leather gloves against his thigh in irritation. His jaw was clenched and the dark look on his face was currently directed at Dalton. She had seen that look before.

One day four years ago at Robin's bar. She was out with Rachel, and a couple of other friends from college celebrating the end of midterms when she spotted his large body slouched at the bar downing a beer. In her slightly inebriated state she felt sexy and strong and she took it upon herself to offer him a night of pleasure.

To her horror and shame, he turned her down flat, barely even looking at her as he broke her heart and bruised her pride. She had been mortified and from that moment she swore she would never offer herself to another man, much less Tanner Keegan. And yet here she was, sitting in his brother's lap, considering letting Dalton seduce her clothes off and show her what a good time he could give her.

Tanner's interruption was the splash of ice water on her face she needed to regain her composure. "Its fine, Tanner, he was just playing around."

"No I wasn't, but I didn't realize that big brother had staked a claim on you already. My apologies," Dalton said with a nod in Tanner's direction. When Tanner nodded in acceptance, Zoey got pissed.

"What? Staked a claim on me? You two have got to be fucking kidding me! Neither of you has any right to stake a claim on me. I'm my own person." She stomped over to Tanner and shoved her index finger into the center of his wide chest. "You! You turned *me* down, not the other way around, buster, so don't even think you stand a chance of staking a claim on this piece of ass." Tanner's eyes widened but his dark look didn't change at all. Spinning around, she pointed at Dalton who threw both hands up in the air, "And you! I haven't seen you in a decade, so don't you dare start throwing out sexy words and flirting. I don't give a crap how lonely you are, you can go back to Africa and fuck a rhino because neither of you are going to seduce me or claim me anytime soon. Got it?"

Her breath was coming in pants as adrenaline rushed through her veins. Who the hell did these two think they were? She wasn't living here to be a temporary lay for a couple of cowboys. In fact, if that's how this was going to play out, she was going to get her stuff and head for her car. She would rather sleep in the backseat for a year than be taken advantage of.

The silence in the room was suffocating, but slowly the tension slipped away with her anger. When she felt a little more in control, she threw her shoulders back and lifted her chin in challenge. Dalton's grin skittered over her nerves, but she didn't snap.

"We got it, Zoey. You aren't interested. Now, we're all going to forget this ever happened and go back to whatever we were doing," Tanner said quietly from behind her. A tingling sensation coursed down her spine at his low and slow cowboy drawl.

"Thank you," she said, letting her head drop slightly. "I am going to run into town to the Mercantile for groceries. Is there anything you want to add to the list?"

"I'll drive. I need to stop by Brooks Pastures to pick up the saddle Mack was fixing for me, and get some fertilizer from The Garden Hut." Tanner turned to look at Dalton pointedly.

"I think I'll just head back out to the west pasture. Maybe check the lines. It feels awfully good to be in a saddle again." He gave Zoey a playful wink and she knew that the subject of her seduction wasn't done yet. She watched as he went back out the front door, letting the screen slam behind him.

"I'm sorry for that, Zoey, if I had known that he would try to..." Tanner stopped and Zoey jerked her gaze back to him.

"Try to what? Seduce me? Do you honestly think that I'm that easy, Tanner? Just because I flirted with you one drunk night at Robin's? Well, I'm not. I've had plenty of experience fending off lonely cowboys trying to get into my bed. I can handle Dalton."

The timer on the stove buzzed and she hurried into the kitchen to pull the bread from the oven. The scent of cinnamon and sugar perfumed the air, and she sighed with pleasure at the golden brown loaf as she put it on the counter.

"You made bread?" Tanner sounded so surprised that she laughed.

"Yes, and chili too. I'm going to grab my purse, and shoes. I want to get back here in time to sneak in an afternoon nap before dinner." Without letting him respond, she headed down the hallway toward her room. There was no way she would ever be able to admit how much of a lie her rant was. She wanted both Keegan cowboys, and the idea of one of them staking a claim on her made her pussy wet and her tits swell.

She knew that it was wrong, but an idea tickled the back of her brain all the same. Dalton lived in the apartment over the garage, which meant that if she made her way into his bed one night, there was no way Tanner would ever know. For a brief moment she considered the same could be said in reverse if she found herself in Tanner's bed, but she nixed that idea quickly. Tanner wasn't interested. He had made that clear. If she wanted to ride a Keegan cowboy, it would have to be Dalton.

---

"So, have you slept with him yet?"

Zoey choked on the gum she was chewing and Rachel handed her a glass of water. "I've only been there one night, Rach! Are you serious?"

Rachel grinned, her brown eyes twinkling. "It took me less than two hours to get naked, so I have a warped frame of reference."

"Yeah, well your men brought you here with the express intent of getting you naked. Tanner doesn't see me as anything more than a younger sister he's responsible for."

"Ha! That's rich!" Rachel laughed loudly, and Zoey glared at her best friend. "You need to open your eyes, woman. That man is hopelessly in lust with you. He looks at you like a steak cooked to perfection on a starving man's plate. I swear I was looking for burn marks on your ass earlier when you guys got here because the hot look in his eyes as he watched you walk away from the truck should have left scars."

"Shut up," Zoey grumbled.

Rachel was seated in a padded rocking chair with Juliet suckling at her breast happily. Zoey couldn't help the surge of jealousy that went through her. It was easy for Rachel to say things like that because she was happily married to four men. No such luck for her best friend. Zoey had a feeling she was destined to a life of being the best friend, and not a wife.

"Does that hurt?" she asked as her curiosity finally got the best of her.

Rachel smiled down at her daughter, "It did at first, but not really anymore. Maybe I got used to it, I don't know. I like being able to breast feed her. It's our alone time without all of the daddies involved."

"But I fed her with a bottle, and I know the guys do too."

Rachel snorted, "Oh yeah, believe me I pump too. Breast milk freezes, and sometimes mommy needs time away from being the milk cow."

Tanner's voice drifted through the front door and Zoey sighed. "I guess that means our visit is over. The Master is calling me."

"You know you can come over any time. Mom might be here, but that doesn't have to stop you from visiting." Rachel gave her a concerned look.

"I know. Wait, where is your mom?"

"Napping. She took Jules for me last night so I could have a whole night of sleep."

Zoey laughed at the blissful look on Rachel's face, "You mean to tell me that with four men in the house you're still the one to get up every night with the baby?"

"Of course. They love Juliet to pieces, but they all sleep like freaking rocks. They wouldn't wake up if the house was burning down."

"Zoey? We need to go." Both women turned as Tanner stepped into the living room. When his eyes landed on Rachel whose boob was unashamedly out for her daughter's feeding, he actually flushed and shuffled awkwardly. "Sorry, Rachel, uh Zoey, we better get going."

"It's okay, Tanner, it's just a boob," Zoey said with a laugh as she waved to Rachel, "I'll call you later this week."

"Sounds good, don't let the job get you down, Zoey. Not when so many other things in your life are looking up," Rachel responded. When Zoey snorted in disagreement Tanner gave her a frown and a questioning look.

There was no way Zoey was going to touch that subject with a ten foot pole so she ignored it and stepped past Tanner onto the front porch. Mack Thompson was standing at the foot of the steps, and Zoey gave him a grin.

"Hey, Mack, I haven't seen you for a while. Where have you been hiding?" she asked the enormous man.

Mack was six foot five and built like a locomotive. He had muscles on top of muscles that should have looked intimidating with the red bandana tied over his blonde curls. Instead, he looked almost angelic when he smiled because his two deep dimples appeared and his crystal clear blue eyes sparkled.

He held his hand out in a gentlemanly fashion to help her down the steps and she giggled but accepted it. "Zoey, aren't you looking beautiful. I actually had to take a quick trip to Chicago to pick up my brother. He managed to hurt himself and needed a place to stay for a bit while he recovered."

"I didn't even know you had a brother, I'm sorry to hear he's injured. What happened?"

"He plays pro football, and he took a hard hit. Tore the ligaments in his shoulder, so he's down for the next eight to twelve weeks," Mack answered.

"Ryker and Sawyer make quite the pair exchanging moans and groans over their injuries," Hudson said as he came out of the barn and stepped closer to the three of them. "Hey, Zoey, I didn't realize you were with Tanner today."

"Hey yourself, handsome. I'm just tagging along. I have to go to the Merc, Tanner doesn't exactly keep his cupboards stocked. So Ryker, huh? I'll have to make up a casserole for you two bachelors and drop it off to say hello," she said, smiling up at Mack.

Beside her she felt Tanner tense from head to toe, and she had to bite back a laugh. Maybe there was something to what Rachel said. Tanner seemed slightly jealous of the attention she was giving Mack, and she wondered how he would feel if she actually pursued the big man.

"Ryk would love that I'm sure."

"Good, then I'll stop by one evening later this week. I better go now before Tanner turns purple. I seem to be frustrating him to no end lately. Bye, guys." She headed for the truck without saying another word to Tanner and hefted herself up into the seat while he said his goodbyes.

They were nearly to town before either of them spoke.

"Do you have a thing for Mack?"

Zoey was stunned that he asked, and she turned to stare at his profile. His knuckles were white where he gripped the steering wheel, and his jaw was clenched, but otherwise there was no expression on his face.

"I don't know. He's good looking that's for sure. Why do you care?"

Tanner grimaced, "I guess I don't."

After a few more moments he turned and met her eyes. "I care."

Just like that, he stole all of the air from her lungs. She felt warm and cold all over, and her stomach flipped over. "Why?"

"Zoey, I didn't mean to hurt you at Robin's that night. You were drunk, and it wouldn't have been right for me to take advantage of you. You deserved better."

Zoey's back went up, "I deserved to be shot down? Embarrassed? Shamed in front of half the county? Yeah, great, thanks. I'm so glad you were trying to do the right thing."

"Stop, don't be like that. I really was trying to be a decent guy."

"You wouldn't even look at me, Tanner. How is that being a good guy?"

Tanner's eyes flashed golden and he gave her a hard look before turning his eyes back to the road and parking the car. Zoey reached for the door handle, but stopped when he grabbed her chin.

"If I had looked at you, you would have been able to see the truth on my face. You would have seen how much I wanted to scoop you up in my arms and cart you away to my bed. You would have known that I was desperate to peel those skintight jeans off your sexy ass and taste you. That all I could think about was sinking my cock into your tight pussy and fucking you until you screamed my name. That's why I didn't look at you. I had to be strong, because in that moment, you were weak."

Tanner's hand dropped and he flung his truck door open launching himself out of the cab. Zoey watched as he extracted a credit card from his wallet and stomped into the small grocery store with it. Once he was out of view, she slowly climbed out of the truck herself, wobbling on legs that were distinctly unsteady.

Tanner wanted her. Not just for a housekeeper and cook, he said he wanted to sleep with her. It was music to her ears, and yet she had no clue how she should proceed. Should she beg him to carry out his illicit fantasies, or pretend he never spoke them?

She was just stepping into the shop when he reached the door to leave. "I took care of whatever the bill is already with Hal, so just get whatever we need and I'll be waiting in the truck when you're done."

Then he was gone, disappeared down the sidewalk to The Garden Hut. Leaving her stunned and horny in the middle of the only grocery in town as though he had never spoken those life changing words. What a disaster her life was turning out to be.

Sighing heavily, she forced herself to complete her shopping, grimacing as the total appeared on the cash register. The owner of the Mercantile, Hal McCrite, gave her a wink and a smile as he input Tanner's payment information and helped bag her purchases.

"So you're living on the Triple T then, are ya?" Hal was a portly man in his late sixties who had a handlebar mustache and three chins. He was kind, but nosey, and everyone knew he had a thing for Dottie who owned the Ice Cream Shoppe.

"Yes, temporarily. My building was one of the ones bought up by Schmidt." She turned away to help put the groceries back into the small cart, hoping he would drop it.

Of course he didn't, and Zoey felt a hot blush creep over her cheeks when he said, "I didn't realize you and Tanner had taken up."

"We haven't "taken up". He's just a friend helping another friend out of a tight spot."

Hal's smile spread eclipsed only by the long ends of his mustache that desperately needed trimming. "Sure, sure. I understand. Have a nice day, Zoey."

Zoey shoved the cart in front of her, declining the bag boys offer to help. She'd had more than enough help for the day. All she wanted to do was go back to the relative privacy of the Triple T, and hope everyone in Stone River forgot about her. It wasn't until she was out the door and in front of Tanner's truck that his words whispered through her brain again. He eased out of the driver's seat and over to her side to help load the groceries into the back of the truck.

"Jesus, did you leave anything in the store?" he muttered and Zoey's temper cracked.

"Well maybe I would have if you'd had anything in your God Damn kitchen besides meat. Humans aren't able to survive on meat alone, you know? And where do you get off saying something like that to me and then just climbing out of the car like it wasn't anything. You don't work a girl up and then walk away. It's just plain wrong. Did you ever stop to think about how I felt? Did you ever consider that maybe what you wanted was the same damn thing I wanted? Huh?" By the end of her tirade Zoey's voice had risen several octaves, and Tanner's eyelids had lowered until he glared at her through narrow slits.

She glanced around her, seeing for the first time that there were several people standing on the sidewalk listening to her tantrum. Embarrassment flooded her and she dropped her head.

"Shit. I'm sorry."

"I should hope so. Get in the truck, and we'll continue this conversation at home," Tanner's voice was hard, and his demand was cold.

Zoey hurried to do what she was told praying that she hadn't just screwed up the smidge of a chance she had with Tanner. After he opened up to her, she had no right to yell at him like that.

The two of them rode home in complete silence, and Tanner unloaded all of the groceries alone while growling at her to stay out of his way. She chose to remain quiet as she put the food away, still wondering if he would address it, or pretend it never happened.

When she shut the cabinet door for the last time, she let out a groan of frustration. Her eyes were burning with the need to have a good cry, but she refused to give in to it. Turning around, she let out a gasp of surprise finding Tanner standing a few feet behind her watching her.

She stared up into his hard expression and swallowed hard when he started to move closer.

"What do you want, Zoey?" he asked softly from only inches away. The tips of her breasts brushed against his chest, and even though there were several layers of fabric between them, she felt them harden.

"What do you mean?" she stammered, staring up at his lips. She couldn't drag her eyes away from them.

"You asked me if I ever considered what you wanted, so now I'm asking you. What do you want?"

Her mouth dropped open, but she wasn't able to force out words.

"Come on. Where's that bravado you had back in town?" The corner of his lips curled up in a mocking smile and she went for broke.

"Kiss me."

His sharp inhale and flaring nostrils were the only indication that she caught him off guard. He hesitated only a moment before dropping his mouth to capture hers in a hard lip lock.

Fire coursed through her veins as his mouth moved on hers, branding her and making her ache. It blew her fantasies out of the water, and she clung to him. Her arms wrapped around his neck as he pressed her back into the cabinets. She could feel his thumbs pressing into her hips just above her hipbones. If he held her any tighter she would have bruises in the morning.

His tongue slid past the barrier of her teeth to dance with hers, and she moaned into his mouth, opening wider to give him access. She could feel the hard length of his cock pressing against her stomach and she rubbed against him like a cat on a scratching post. Just when she was ready to shuck her clothes and fuck like rabbits on the kitchen counter, his hands fell away and he stepped backwards.

Zoey swayed on her feet and made a little whimpering sound of protest as she struggled to come back to earth. One look at Tanner and her heart plummeted. His jaw worked, and his now kiss swollen lips were tight with tension.

"Shit, I shouldn't have done that."

"What?" She stared up at him praying that he wasn't regretting such a spectacular moment. Her worst fears were confirmed when he pushed away from her several steps.

"Christ, I know better. I need to get out of here." And he was gone.

Zoey stood there for several minutes in shock before she slid to the floor and buried her face in her hands to have a much needed cry.

Just when she thought she was making progress with Tanner, he had to go and fuck it up. God, she could just throttle him sometimes. Leaving her horny and pissed off was not in his best interests when she was the one cooking his dinner. The moment the thought crossed her mind she let out an emotional laugh. No matter what he did to push her buttons, she cared about him way too much to consider hurting him back.

Pushing herself off the floor, she headed for her room. If she was going to be miserable with her hurt feelings, then she would at least be sexually satisfied. Masturbation was rapidly becoming her favorite pastime.

## CHAPTER SIX

Clint Keegan took a taxi home from the airport. It was bad enough he had to come home with his tail between his legs. He wasn't about to be trapped in a vehicle listening to his oldest brother telling him "I told you so" all the way back.

For twelve years he had flirted with fame in Hollywood. Bit parts, the occasional commercial, but nothing meaty came his way. He dated actresses and models, but he was one of the thousands that never were discovered. Oh sure, he had an agent who thought he was the next Tom Cruise or Brad Pitt, but only until he couldn't pay his fee anymore. Then it was "Hit the road kid, you aren't cut out for this business."

When he took off for California at eighteen, he knew he was destined for fame. Everyone told him that he had a movie star face, and he had starred in all of the community theater programs at home. He figured if he didn't land a great movie deal right away, he could always pose for a few magazines or catalogues to get by. What he hadn't counted on was the competition. In Stone River, Texas, there was no competition. In Los Angeles, California, every waitress, bus boy, hotel clerk, and phone operator was a star in waiting.

The promise he made to his mother a few years ago when pops had his heart attack had snuck up on him. Now he was thirty, and he knew in his heart that his acting days were over. In truth, he was tired of the game. He missed home, but he would never admit that to his family. Not that it would make a difference. They always thought he was a dreamer, and his choice to run away to be an actor solidified that assumption for them.

Clint hadn't even spoken to Tanner in six or eight months. Hell, he hadn't talked to Dalton in almost a year other than the occasional email. A heavy ball of guilt sat in his gut. It was as much his fault as theirs. He hadn't wanted to admit to them that he was still a struggling actor when they were doing so well. Dalton was a doctor, and Tanner owned the ranch for fucks sake. Clint was just the failure who could make people laugh.

The sun was low and his belly was growling as he paid the cab, then retrieved his suitcase. Standing in front of his childhood home, he was flooded with memories of playing basketball behind the barn, shooting BB guns at tin cans from the front porch, Christmases and Easters and everything in between. The smell of home hit him as he pulled the front door open. It was still exactly as it had been when his parents lived there, and he was comforted by that. Maybe being home wouldn't be so terrible.

Of course, in all likelihood, Tanner didn't have the extra resources to redecorate, but still, his mother would be pleased he had left it the way she had it, if she came home for Christmas. A noise in the kitchen surprised him, and he lowered his bag to the floor before walking through the living room. Expecting to find Tanner microwaving a frozen dinner, he was shocked to find a sexy woman dancing around the kitchen with a bowl in her hands and ear buds in her ears. She was humming a tune Clint recognized from the radio and stirring whatever was in her bowl like a mad woman.

Her long dark hair drifted around her swaying hips as she grooved to the music, and Clint couldn't take his eyes off her ass. Perfectly shaped with just enough junk in the trunk to make it soft. It made his mouth water.

He wondered what the rest of her looked like, and when she continued to work with the goop in her bowl like she hadn't heard him, he figured he better announce himself. Reaching out, he plucked one of the black ear buds from her ear, and said, "How did Tanner manage to catch an angel and put her to work in his kitchen?"

Instead of laughing, the woman screamed and Clint found himself covered in white icing from nipples to nose as the bowl she had been holding flew at him.

"Holy shit, angel! I wanted a taste, but I didn't need to wear it!"

The woman stood across the kitchen with both hands over her mouth. She had mesmerizing cornflower blue eyes that were wide with shock, and then crinkling with laughter as she began to giggle. Clint should have been pissed, but the soft sound of her giggles went straight to his cock making him hard as concrete.

"Clint? Oh my God! I didn't know you were coming home!" She went to the sink to collect a washcloth and wet it before hurrying to his side. "I'm so sorry! I can't believe I threw that at you! Here, let me help."

Her tiny hands began running over his face, neck, and chest as she attempted to wipe the creamy goop from his skin. His mouth quirked up in a grin when he finally realized who was giving him a sponge bath. "Zoey Carson?"

She froze and lifted those beautiful blue eyes to his, "Yes, but I'm surprised you remembered me."

"Oh I never forget a gorgeous face. So how did Tanner manage to land you? Last I knew he was living like a priest, paying more attention to his land than his dick." Clint took the cloth she held out and completed the job before using paper towels to dry his face. His shirt was sticky, so he tugged it off over his head. Awareness zipped through him when her eyes zeroed in on his cut chest. He might not have made any movies, but he still had a movie star body thanks to the ten hours a day he had been putting in as a landscaper for the last couple of years.

"Uh...um...Tanner didn't land me. I'm just living with him, er...well... temporarily. He's giving me a place to stay for a couple of weeks. Does he know you're back? He didn't say anything to me." Zoey seemed flustered as she retrieved the now empty bowl and put it in the sink to be washed. He watched as she pulled another bowl from the cabinet and began making the icing again.

"Not yet, but he'll know soon enough. So you're not Tanner's girl then?"

She hesitated before shaking her head no, and Clint was intrigued. They might not be an official couple, but something was up between the two of them.

"Well good, then I don't have to feel bad about making out with you." He turned and started to walk back to the living room, working hard to resist laughing at her gasp and fumbling protest.

"Wait a second, I'm not making out with you!" She looked so indignant that he wanted to throw her to the floor and prove her wrong. Instead he just shrugged.

"No, not yet. We'll save that for later. First, I need to unload my stuff in my room. Do you know where I can find Tanner?" Clint stopped and cocked his head in confusion because her cheeks went pale.

"Your room? Um...well...you can't."

"I can't? I can't what?" He narrowed his eyes.

"You can't use your room."

A laugh burst from his throat, "Oh really? And why is that?"

"Um, because I'm using it."

Clint was struck dumb. He stood there staring at her, and fighting to keep his erection from busting the seams of his pants. Holy fuck! The angel was sleeping in his bed! How lucky could he get? He knew he should be a gentleman and offer to take the couch, but if Zoey wasn't with anyone right now, then he wanted to take advantage of this moment and coax her into giving him a shot. He couldn't wait to get her under him naked.

When he left years ago, she had just started puberty. She was skinny as a rail and her head was bigger than the rest of her. Now, she was a voluptuous woman with killer porn star curves. It reminded him of his own ugly duckling phase, and it shouldn't surprise him that she had matured into a swan too.

"Aw, that's alright, Zoey love. That will save me some time and effort, because you were going to end up there eventually anyway." He spun on his heel as she sputtered and cursed up a blue streak behind him.

Laughter spilled from his chest, but he kept walking toward the living room to get his stuff. Clint wasn't the type to force a woman, but he would sure as hell seduce her. *Watch out Zoey Carson, I've got you in my sites, and I'm planning on bagging the trophy*, as he put his luggage into his now shared bedroom.

Maybe coming home wouldn't be as bad as he thought.

His bedroom smelled sweet, a blend of him and Zoey. The scent didn't help the erection he was trying to ignore as he set his gear in one corner and pulled on a clean shirt. Before looking for his brothers, he peeked around. She didn't have much, a few things in the dresser drawers, a cedar chest, a bike, and a framed photo of her and another woman sat on the bedside table next to a romance novel.

Clint did a double take when he saw the couple on the cover weren't just embracing. The woman was bound with rope, and blindfolded, while the man hovered near her ear holding her close.

The knowledge that Zoey didn't mind a little kink in her play sent his temperature skyrocketing. He had to shake himself hard to get his brain functioning again.

*What the fuck is wrong with you, Keegan? You haven't even been home for a full hour and you already want to seduce a local and tie her to the bed so she can't get away. You don't even know her!*

With that thought firmly in his brain, his cock began to slowly deflate until he was able to walk more comfortably. Now that he was thinking properly again, it was time to find his big brother and swallow his pride.

He glanced toward the kitchen on his way to the front door, but Zoey was nowhere in sight. A twinge of disappointment was ignored as he walked across the yard to the open barn doors. It felt strange to be walking into the barn in tennis shoes and not cowboy boots, but oddly, the familiar smells and warmth of the old building were comforting.

Standing in the middle of the aisle with his back to him was Tanner. He was talking to someone, and when Clint heard a female's distinct huff of irritation, he knew he had found the missing Zoey.

What he wasn't prepared for, was to find Dalton as well.

"Professor?"

All three turned to look at him, and Dalton's face broke out in a wide grin. "Gilligan! Damn, boy, it's good to see you!"

Clint hugged his brother, clapping him on the back and fighting the emotions that welled up inside of him. He and Dalton had always been the closest of the three brothers. Maybe it was because they were the younger two, or maybe they just understood the other's need to escape Texas and the pressure of the ranch.

Pulling back from Dalton, he turned to Tanner, "Skipper! Wow, do you know how much you look like pops?"

"Fuck you too, Hollywood!" Tanner said, but his lips quirked up in a half smile as he held his hand out for a handshake. Clint jerked his grip and hugged his older brother loosely.

"Hollywood, huh? Well, it's better than Gilligan."

Zoey cleared her throat, but the moment they all three turned their attention on her she looked like a deer in the headlights, shifting nervously on her feet. "Um, yeah, so it's great that we're having a family reunion and all the name calling, but uh, there's kind of the problem of three beds and four people."

Clint reached out and snagged her around the waist, determined to shake her of the prim and proper way she set her spine when she spoke to him. "I told you, angel. I don't mind sharing. I'll keep your back warm…or your front, I'm not picky."

She planted her two tiny hands on his muscular chest and pushed. If he hadn't released her she wouldn't have been able to move him, but he let her go easily. "I am not sharing a bed with you, Clint. I'm happy you're home for your brother's sake, but I'm not a welcome home gift."

"You can share mine, pretty lady," Dalton said with a chuckle, and Clint gave him a fist bump.

"Shut up both of you jackasses. Zoey isn't going to be sharing anyone's bed. Just because I turned my old room into an office doesn't mean I wasn't thinking we would all be back here at some point. The sofa in there pulls out into a bed. Clint can sleep in there." Tanner nodded to Zoey who gave him a smile that almost took Clint's breath away. She was absolutely radiant.

Her beauty didn't distract him enough that he wouldn't argue a little, "Hey! Why am I the one giving up my bed?"

"Because it hasn't been your bed for years. It's Zoey's bed now. Enough about beds," Tanner adjusted his stance and Clint almost laughed out loud. So, he was right that there was attraction between Zoey and his oldest brother, he just didn't realize that Dalton was in the running too. This could end up being an interesting foot race.

"So, are you back for good, little brother?" Dalton asked, taking a seat on a hay bale nearby. He patted his knee and held out his hand for Zoey, who rolled her eyes and shook her head.

"Yep. I think so. I'm not sure what I'm going to do back here, but my Hollywood dreams died on my thirtieth birthday. What about you, Professor? What are you doing out of the wilds of Africa? Did your rhino girlfriend leave you high and dry and you came home to nurse a broken heart?"

Dalton flipped him off. "I see you're still a dickwad. MSF actually shut down the program in Somalia. I didn't have another post to go to, so I came home for a while. Tanner needed a hand on the ranch, and rumor has it that Doc Plass might want to retire soon."

Clint felt his mouth drop open, "You mean you might stay for good?"

Dalton just shrugged.

"I think I'm going to just leave you three to catch up. I have to make another batch of icing for the bread," Zoey said, turning to leave.

"Another batch?" Tanner questioned.

"I ended up wearing the first batch. It was pretty damn tasty though, angel. Just give me more notice the next time you want to play with food, and I'll make sure I start out naked." He winked at her, and enjoyed the slight pink flush that stained her cheeks before she stomped out of the barn, her heart shaped ass swaying. When she disappeared out the doors, Clint turned just in time to realize both of his brothers' eyes had been locked on her ass too.

Locking that tidbit of info away for the moment, he pulled on a more serious face. "How did you end up with a woman living here that you can't fuck?"

Matching hard looks from both Dalton and Tanner surprised him, and he held his hands up, "Sorry! I just wanted to know what the story was."

"Zoey needed a place to stay, so I gave her one. She is under my protection, so don't push her too hard. She's not one of your bimbo California women," Tanner said, giving him a glare.

"Gotcha. You have a thing for her. I don't blame you, but I won't make any promises. If she gives me a signal, all bets are off. That woman is hot as hell, and based on her reading material, I think she has a kinky side I would love to explore," Clint said just as seriously.

Dalton perked up, "Kinky side?"

"The book on the night table in my old room certainly isn't a children's book," Clint said with a laugh.

"Her choice of reading material is her business. Lay off, Clint," Tanner snapped.

"Got it, Skipper. So, tell me what's been going on at the ranch." The three men settled in to catch up, and Clint finally felt like he could breathe again. This was home, and this was how home was supposed to be. The three of them together again, talking horses, woman, and beer. It had been years since he felt like he belonged somewhere, and he was glad it was here.

---

Zoey was really irritated. Who the hell did Clint Keegan think he was? Good grief, these Keegan cowboys were as arrogant and cocksure as any prize bull in the pen. By the time she had dinner ready she had no appetite for anything but chewing cowboy ass. There was no way she could tolerate the flirting, kissing, and teasing from all three of them.

After Tanner left her high and dry in the kitchen, she had gone in and taken an hour nap to recover her sanity. Of course she had masturbated twice too, but that was just to take the edge off her temper...or so she told herself.

She was on her way to forgiving and forgetting the incident when Clint scared the shit out of her in the kitchen while she was making icing to drizzle over the cinnamon bread. His arrogance had lit the fire under her mad again out in the barn. Between Dalton's open flirting, Clint's arrogance, and Tanner's brooding, she was piping hot and ready to blow by dinnertime. Half mad and half horny didn't make a good combination when she had to face off with all of them.

The three men came out of the barn as a unit, and Zoey felt her lungs tighten and her mouth go dry as she stood on the front porch watching them saunter toward her, laughing as brothers. Clint's appearance in Stone River wasn't all that much of a surprise to Tanner and Dalton.

He was the youngest, but he was slightly taller than Tanner and Dalton, although it was hard to tell when he was the only one without a hat on. Ever since he hit puberty he had been good looking, but he had aged to perfection after high school, and she was honestly shocked that he hadn't made it big in Hollywood.

Seeing the trio all together, she instantly had thoughts of a wild group orgy. She could envision them stripping her down right here on the front porch and having their wicked way with her.

*Good grief, Rachel's four husbands have skewed my sense of reality.*

Even though her panties were damp and her nipples were aching, she forced a frown to her face and crossed her arms over her chest. The three men quieted when they drew closer to her. Clint had a wicked grin on his face, Dalton looked slightly confused by her annoyance, and Tanner just refused to meet her gaze.

"So it's one big happy family then?" she asked in the bratty tone she knew irritated Tanner.

Clint threw an arm around each brother's shoulders and laughed. "Yep, come on over here and we'll have a group hug, angel."

Zoey rolled her eyes and spun around to go back in the house.

"Even better, I like it when you walk away from me. Then I get to see that ripe ass," Clint called out. His gasp of pain when one of his brothers—probably Tanner—elbowed him in the gut, gave Zoey a small measure of satisfaction. "Fuck you too, Skipper. You don't have to maim me because you have a hard-on for her too."

She made her legs move a little faster as a hot blush stole up her cheeks. The idea of any one of the three brothers having a hard-on for her drove her body temperature sky high. The sensation of Tanner's cock against her belly was scorched into her brain, and she couldn't stop herself from wondering about the size of his brothers erections.

As she went to lift the heavy pot of chili from the stove, she felt warmth at her back, and two muscular arms stopped her. Looking over her shoulder, she found Dalton inches from her backside, and she let out a little gasp. "I got it, Zoey. Sit down."

His lips just barely brushed by her ear before she ducked under his arm and hurried to carry the bread to the table. Clint had taken the seat next to hers, and Tanner was at the head of the table, which left Dalton to sit across from her. She was surrounded by the three of them again, and it made her head swim a bit.

"So, Zoey, how did you end up living at the Triple T?" Clint asked as he reached for her bowl and dished chili into it as if he did it every day. She stared at the bowl for a moment of pure fascination before remembering her manners and thanking him.

"It's a long story," she said noncommittally while helping herself to a slice of bread.

"I have nothing but time," Clint answered with a laugh right before sinking his teeth into his bread. He moaned with pleasure and she smiled at his reaction. Arrogant ass or not, she liked seeing people enjoy her cooking.

"A developer bought the building I was living in, forcing me to look for a new place, and then my mom stole all of my money so I couldn't put a deposit down on the only house for rent in town. That left me high and dry with only a few days left to figure out where to stay."

"Damn. I'm sorry I asked, angel. I didn't mean to upset you." Clint looked genuinely apologetic and she shrugged at him.

"Everyone in Stone River knows my parents are worthless. I guess I'm just a glutton for punishment. She showed up asking to stay at my place and then she disappeared one night along with all of the money in my bank account." Dalton reached across the table and squeezed Zoey's hand giving her a reassuring smile.

"I for one am glad she left. It sucks that she took your money and hurt you, but I'm not sure when I would have gotten to see you if you hadn't ended up here at the Triple T." She gave Dalton a small smile of thanks before turning back to Clint.

"I was planning on staying with Rachel and her husbands, but they just had a baby, and then Sawyer had to have surgery on his knee—"

"Wait, husbands? Did you say Rachel and her husbands? Rachel Morgan had a baby. With Sawyer? As in Brooks?" Clint's mouth hung open in surprise and even Tanner laughed at his expression.

"Yes she did, now shut your trap before the bees start building a hive in there," Tanner said shaking his head.

"Holy shit, it's like I've died and gone to heaven. I come home to find a sexy angel is sleeping in my bed and people are embracing group love! Why did I ever leave Stone River?"

"To be a star!" Dalton answered with a dramatic wave of his arms.

Clint snorted, "Yeah that didn't work out so well."

Zoey frowned at him, "But you were in several commercials. I even saw the dog food one a few times."

Suddenly the cock-sure man was a sad and dejected little boy, and Zoey's heart broke a little. She had to scoop food into her mouth to keep from putting an arm around him to comfort him.

"Unfortunately that is my only claim to fame. I never managed to break into the biz. I spent more time bussing tables and mowing lawns than acting. So tell me about Rachel and Sawyer and her other husbands."

"Rachel legally married Rogan Brooks, but they had a commitment ceremony between all four brothers and her. She just had a baby girl a couple of months ago, Juliet." Zoey explained, she felt Tanner's eyes on her as she chatted with Clint, but she made no move to acknowledge it. Her pride was still stinging from his rejection earlier.

"How in the world did that happen? And why?" Clint asked with a frown.

Zoey giggled, "I'm pretty sure it happens the way all relationships happen. They fell in love. Actually, I think they fell in lust first. They invited her to have a weekend fling with them one Friday night, and by Sunday, the guys were pledging their undying love. Rachel took a bit more convincing, but once she accepted her own feelings, it was like they were always meant to be together. Those four guys make great dads too."

"I never pictured Parker Brooks cooing at a baby, but trust me, he does," Tanner said, with a wry grin on his face.

"He's not the only one," Zoey said, and when Dalton and Clint looked at her in question she gestured to Tanner with her fork, "Your big brother is wrapped around that baby girl's finger too, trust me, I've seen it in person."

"Things sure have changed around here," Clint said, shaking his head.

The conversation turned to less personal questions. Everyone seemed to avoid talking about the past and the future. Preferring to stay on fluff topics like town gossip and the tasks that had to be done over the next week on the ranch.

By the end of dinner the three brothers seemed to have made a silent agreement to ignore the past between them, and start fresh. Zoey was the only outsider.

As usual, she was the one with no links to the past, and no solid leads to her future. The three brothers continued their easy conversation and insisted on cleaning up the kitchen since she cooked, so she silently slipped away leaving them to it.

Her legs carried her outside and down the road a ways before she stopped and took a seat on a tree stump to stare up at the sky. Worries bounced in her brain making her stomach tight and her heart heavy.

She still had no idea where her mother was, or if she was okay. Eve's cell phone number had been disconnected, so even if she wanted to leave a message she couldn't. Tomorrow she had to return to work and admit that she was at the bottom of the dung heap, and she still had absolutely no idea where she was going to live permanently.

How had things spiraled out of control so quickly in her life? It seemed like just days ago she was graduating, celebrating the successful completion of her life's goal, and planning a brilliant entry into the career world. The reality sure paled in comparison to the fantasy she'd had in her mind back then.

Staring up into the inky black sky, she searched instinctively for specific constellations. There was Orion, and the big dipper, Cassiopeia, and Andromeda. It was a soothing ritual she had when she needed to think, and she was thankful the night was clear and warm.

When movement drew her attention and she turned to find Dalton standing a few feet away, he held two beer bottles in his hand. "Are you alright?"

Forcing a smile she nodded, "Sure. Just enjoying the stars."

He moved closer, handing her a beer and then taking a seat on the ground so his back rested against the stump she sat on and his shoulder pressed against her leg. "Enjoying the stars, or escaping the testosterone?"

She snorted, and then giggled, "Maybe a little of both."

"I can't believe Clint came back. I know he promised mom, but I was stunned to see him today." Dalton's words were quiet, and Zoey had to strain to hear him.

"You? I was the one he scared half to death. He's lucky I had a bowl of icing and not the bread knife in my hands, or you would have been planning a funeral," she said sarcastically. He turned to look up at her, his gorgeous smile lit by the moonlight, and she sighed with longing. Her hand itched to run through his blonde hair, loosening if from where his cowboy hat had pressed it down. Instead, she began picking at the sticker on her beer bottle.

"That's just it, huh?"

"What do you mean?"

"The planning. We're all at a stage where we're supposed to be planning our futures. Laying out a course for ourselves, a flawless path to happiness if you will. We should be capable of overcoming the skeletons in our closets and forgiving all of the hurts from the past, so we can have a bright future. Instead, you and I are drinking beer in the moonlight in the middle of a Texas ranch, and neither of us knows what the fuck tomorrow will hold."

"Amen," she said, laughing just a little. They sat in silence for a while, enjoying the quiet and their own thoughts. "So what kind of plan have you come up with, Doctor?"

"Hmm…I still think my first step should be seducing you into my bed, because then it will be much easier to convince you to spend the rest of your life cooking your delicious food for me, and driving my brothers crazy that they don't have you." He responded to her glare of disapproval with a wink, and then shrugged, "Or, I can head back inside to obtain more beer and we can sit here until morning watching the moon move across the sky."

She couldn't help but laugh. He was as big of a flirt as the other two, but there seemed to be something deeper in him tonight. There was a missing piece to the puzzle that was Dalton Keegan, and she grew more intrigued every minute she spent with him.

"I could spend hours staring at the sky searching for answers and still have no idea what's next." She could hear the wistful sadness in her own voice, so she knew Dalton could too.

"What's holding you back?" he asked, without moving a muscle to look away from the sky.

She sighed, "My past I suppose. Or maybe my fear of the past repeating itself. I wanted my degree so badly because I wanted to be able to help other kids. I need to make sure they know that it gets better, and that their circumstances when they are young don't define them when they are adults."

"A lofty goal. I know you and I haven't spent a lot of time together, and we weren't close before I left, but somehow I just know you can achieve that if you are determined to. Skeletons can be pretty motivating."

The fact that he understood what she was saying without her having to explain it made her relax her guard a little more. It was as sure sign she should stand up and walk back into the house as quickly as possible but instead, she heard words coming out of her mouth. "So what skeletons are you trying to overcome?"

"Do you really want to know?" he asked, tipping his head and looking at her thoughtfully. When she nodded, he slowly rose to his feet, and held out his hand. "Come on, I think better when I'm moving."

She let him help her up, and they left their half empty bottles on the stump to retrieve later, before slowly walking down the road away from the house. It was several moments before he spoke, but when he did the sadness in his voice strangled her heart.

"I know you didn't have a great childhood here. It's a small town, so I heard the rumors, and after your mom's recent stunt, I have a pretty good idea of what life has been like for you. For me though, Stone River was a great place to grow up. I was lucky enough to have a great family, and a lot of freedom. Part of that freedom was that I could run wild with my best friend, Ben White. We were double trouble, believe me. I can't even tell you how many times the Sherriff picked us up causing problems for one of the local businesses and took us home. One of our favorite things to do during the summer was to go swimming at Devil's Drop."

"Devil's Drop? That place is a national park or something, isn't it?" Zoey frowned at him, and tucked her hair behind her ear.

"It is now, but it wasn't back then. You were probably only 4 or 5 when it happened...God that makes me feel old." He stopped moving and his head dropped dramatically.

"When *what* happened?"

"Ben and I went swimming one afternoon, just like always. Jumping off the rocks into the pool. You know, the thing about Devil's Drop is that it's spring fed from an underground cave system. The pool itself is almost fifty feet deep, or so I've been told." He started walking again, but he seemed to have forgotten she was with him. She stayed quiet, listening to his story, and fearing she knew how it ended. "Ben was a great kid. He got straight As, he was the star of the little league team, and he was a loyal friend."

There were several more breaths between them, where the only sound was the crunching of grass under their feet. Dalton's tone changed when he spoke again, dropping an octave and filling with emotion. "He jumped off the rocks one last time. We had to go home because his mama was going to take us shopping for fireworks. We were eleven-year-old boys, so we loved shooting off fireworks and the stands had just opened for the season. Before we could go, Ben wanted to jump just one more time. I climbed out and I was drying off when he went in. He slipped as he got to the top of the rock, and fell. His head cracked against the granite before he tumbled into the pool. I could see the blood spray from his forehead when he hit, and then he was gone. Disappeared under the water. Just like that. I panicked, and took off for help when he didn't come back up. I never even went in the water to see if I could save him."

Dalton stopped moving and stared up into the dark sky. His body was so tense he looked like he would snap like a rubber band if she touched him, but she chanced it. Wrapping her arms around him, she held him against her, trying to absorb his pain. He tensed only for a moment, before his arms came up to clutch her to him. He pressed his face against the top of her head and continued his story.

"It took divers to find his body, and the autopsy said he died of blunt force trauma. He was dead before he went into the water, but I didn't know that. He was my best friend and I never even went into the water to try to help him. I ran away. What kind of a coward runs away and leaves his best friend behind?"

"Dalton, you were only a kid. You couldn't have gotten him out alone even if you had been able to reach him."

"Oh I know. I'm a doctor after all. I know that it was a hopeless situation, but in my heart, I can't forgive myself. After that, every time I ran into his mom, Minnie, she would see me and start crying. She couldn't even stand to speak to me. His dad, Walt, would move to the other side of the road to avoid me. So I knew when I was eleven that I would have to leave Stone River behind. There was no way I could face what I had done, or make Walt and Minnie relive it for the rest of their lives. I left. I went to med school and after med school I found the program that would send me the furthest possible distance from Texas. Like any good coward, I kept running hoping I could outrun my past. I feel like I've been running for twenty years, ever since I turned away from Ben. Until two weeks ago, when my program was shut down and I was shipped back. Now I'm just trying to figure out how to take it all in, and what to do next."

They held each other in silence. Zoey tried to put all of the compassion she had in her heart into that hug, and Dalton seemed to absorb it readily. His hand stroked her hair gently, as though petting her to calm her, but she knew he was really doing it to soothe the turmoil inside of himself. She began running her own hands up and down the hard line of his back, trying to give him the comfort he sought. When he leaned back to look down at her, she gave him a small smile. "How about we go in and get that second beer you promised me, then maybe we can see how good you are at the seduction part of your plan?"

"I don't want you to sleep with me out of pity, Zoey. I like you, and you mean more than that to me," he said, shaking his head.

"How can you say that? You barely know me," she argued, pulling her arms away and crossing them over her chest protectively. She couldn't help but feel stung by the rejection.

"I know more than you think. You're a brave, strong woman, with a big heart, and a huge capacity for love. You've been hurt in the past, but that doesn't stop you from helping the ones that have hurt you, and you're in love with my brother." His last words were like a slap to her face, and Zoey took a step backwards.

"What?"

He shrugged, "It's plain as day to me, and a few days ago, I would have never considered making a play for the woman my brother wants as his own, but hearing about Rachel, and the guys, well...it just has me thinking."

"Stop it. Right now. Don't start getting it in your head that just because I'm living here with the three of you, that we're all going to suddenly fall madly in love with each other. You three are mostly jerks, who are cocky and a pain in my neck. Why would I ever want to be saddled with one of you, much less all three of you?" She was breathing hard, but she wasn't sure if it was because what he said made her nervous or turned on.

"Why? Oh that's the easy part. Because, Zoey, sweetheart, we can give you this..." His head dipped, and she had a second where she knew exactly what he was going to do, but she couldn't stop it. She wanted him to kiss her. In fact, she had almost a desperate urge to fuse her mouth to his to prove to both of them that there was no chemistry.

Her plan backfired, because the moment their lips met, electricity sparked in the air and coursed through her body. She moaned as he took the kiss deeper, cupping her jaw with his hands to hold her in place and making love to her mouth. Her body melted into him, and she moaned when he nipped her lip before pulling back with a deep sigh.

"Yep. I knew it. You taste like the perfect sin, woman. Now, are we going to take this up to my bed and continue it, or are you going to walk away?"

He was challenging her. Fire lit the depths of his blue eyes, and she could feel the flush that covered her own neck and chest. Her body wanted his, there was no doubt about it, but she couldn't take the next step with Dalton, until she resolved her feelings for Tanner. Polyamory might work for the Brooks family, but everyone around knew that Zoey Carson was better off alone.

Pushing away from him, she shook her head to clear the lust, and then glared at him. "I'm going to walk away, because like you said, I don't want to be wanted out of pity or some misplaced desire for a future. In a couple of weeks I will move out, and in a couple of months you will leave Stone River, so there is no point in starting something neither one of us have any intention of finishing." She turned and took a few steps toward the house before his voice stopped her for a moment.

"You can run, Zoey, but you can't hide. There is something special between us, and I know it's there between you and Tanner too. I don't know about Clint, but something tells me that fate wouldn't have brought the four of us together in this moment in time, if it weren't for a damn good reason. Good night, Zoey."

Doubling her speed, she let the dark swallow him up behind her as she booked it for the well-lit ranch house. She wasn't sure what she needed right now. Space, time, a good hard fuck? Maybe a little of everything. Dalton's words hit too close to what she herself had been thinking, and it scared the hell out of her.

She wasn't like Rachel. There was no happy ending in the future for broken Zoey. Hadn't she had that proven a dozen times over in just the last month? Besides, once Dalton and Clint spent more time in Stone River they would find someone else to catch their fancy. Some other woman who was prettier and had a lot less baggage. She just needed to focus on finding a new place to live as quickly as possible...and keep her hands off the Keegan threesome.

Easier said than done, a small voice in her brain taunted her as she flew through the front door and straight down the hall to her room.

Locking the door behind her, she dropped onto the bed and let her emotions take over. Her heart broke for Dalton and his dead friend, Ben, for Clint and his broken dreams of acting, and for herself and Tanner, what might have been, but they would never know. It was just one sadness after another, and she found herself sobbing herself to sleep.

## CHAPTER SEVEN

THE NEXT WEEK FLEW BY, and Zoey barely had time to think about her situation, much less lament it. She had always been a morning person, so every day she woke with the sun and made breakfast. It seemed to surprise Tanner that she would meet him in the kitchen for coffee and breakfast. Clint and Dalton would wander in right before she had to go to work, and all three men took the time to wish her a good day. If she didn't know any better, she would almost feel like she belonged there with them.

Work consisted of filling out paperwork, answering phones, filing, and running errands for her bitchy boss, Helen, who she nicknamed, Helga the Hooker. Helen was in her early fifties and a bitter biddy who seemed to have no compassion for the students she worked with. How she ever got a job as a children's social worker was anyone's guess. Zoey knew she was stuck if she wanted to stay in Stone River. Small towns weren't exactly the ideal place for someone in her career, so she forced herself to grin and bear it. According to some of the other staff, the administration was watching her closely to see if she could ultimately be Helen's replacement. It wasn't much, but it was a sliver of hope in her dismal world.

Walking through the front door of the ranch house Friday night, she was assaulted by the scent of garlic and Italian seasonings. Her mouth watered as much as her brain bounced. Every night this week she had come back to the Triple T to cook dinner while the three men worked the ranch. She had been surprised how quickly Clint and Dalton slipped back into their cowboy boots, but they seemed to be enjoying it. The four of them ate dinner and chatted comfortably, although the flirting had continued, it hadn't intensified, and none of the guys had pushed her. After dinner, most of the time she would join one or more of them in the living room to watch TV for an hour or so before she went to bed and masturbated herself to sleep.

Living with them left her perpetually horny. The scent of hay and male sweat was suddenly a powerful aphrodisiac that left her limp with need. If any of them knew the fantasies her brain spun up after she shut her bedroom door, she would be mortified. She attributed her crazy fixation on ménage sex to Rachel's blissful happiness with her men, and it irritated her that she couldn't get off on normal fantasies anymore. Her mind's eye was always adding men to the scene until suddenly she was back to all three Keegan brothers worshipping her body. She was beginning to think she was insane.

To her shock, Clint had taken over the kitchen wearing a white apron that had orange smears of something on it. A large casserole dish sat on the stove and he was layering noodles, sauce, and cheese into it carefully.

"Hey, angel, how was work today?" His smile was wide and welcoming, and she found herself returning it without meaning too.

"Eh, it was work. What in the world are you doing?" she asked, dropping her purse on the counter and removing her earrings.

"Making lasagna. What's it look like?"

She stared at his profile as he worked, enjoying watching the muscles of his forearms flex and roll. "I thought I was supposed to cook?"

He shrugged and winked, "You aren't a servant, Zoey. I wanted you to have a night off, and I actually enjoy cooking."

"Really? Did your mom teach you?" She stepped out of her high heels, scooping them up and hooking them over her purse strap before unbuttoning the top three buttons of her collar. When she glanced back up, Clint's eyes were focused on the exposed skin of her collarbone, and they both swallowed hard.

"Uh, no, actually. I didn't learn until I was in California. I worked as a sous chef for about four years in an Italian restaurant before it went belly up." Zoey watched as he gently pressed noodles into sauce, with the fine precision of a surgeon, and she tingled as she wondered what it would be like to have those same gentle fingers pressing into her skin.

"Thank you. It smells fantastic. Is there anything I can do to help?" She stepped closer and inhaled deeply.

"I'll let you make the bread if you're nice." Clint grinned at her, and then swiped a finger in the sauce and held it to her lips. She hesitated before accepting the challenge in his light brown eyes. They were the color of peanut brittle, and they sparkled when her lips closed over his digit. She ran her tongue over the tip of his finger teasingly before pulling away with a pop.

"Fuck a duck," he groaned, still standing with his finger out as if he couldn't handle pulling it away.

"Tastes delicious," she said softly. "I better go change clothes. I'll help with the garlic bread when I get back."

Turning away, she collected her stuff and left him staring after her. Her step was lighter on her way to the bedroom than when she first came home, and she was fighting to hold in a laugh. How long had it been since someone had done something nice for her, just because? Probably her birthday last spring, when Rachel took her in to Austin for a girl's day of shopping and lunch at her favorite steakhouse. That day turned into a day long shopping spree for Juliet's nursery instead of for Zoey, but it was fun.

Her laundry was piled pretty high, and she grimaced as she realized the only clean lounge clothes she had left was a pair of very short workout shorts, and a slightly too snug t-shirt that showed her belly if she stretched her arms. There really wasn't another option unless she wanted to wear dirty clothes or work clothes all evening. Nixing that option because no woman should have to wear pantyhose more than eight hours a day, she changed and swung her long hair up into a ponytail.

She couldn't have been gone for more than ten minutes, but by the time she reentered the kitchen, Dalton was spreading butter on the French bread, and Clint was topping the lasagna with cheese. They both glanced at her as she came into the room, and froze.

"I like this look," Clint said, eyeing her like a fashion critic, he made a circular motion with his finger so she would spin around and she laughed. The moment her back was to them, she heard them both groan.

"What? Do they look that bad?" She twisted to try to see her own backside, only succeeding in hiking the t-shirt up to show off a band of skin at her midsection.

Dalton put down the butter knife and leaned over to kiss her on the forehead, "Nothing could look bad on you, pretty lady."

A blush stole up her cheeks, and she dropped her eyes. "Thank you, I think. I feel a little useless with the two of you doing the cooking tonight. Is there anything else I can do?"

"Nope, just take a seat and let us handle it. Dinner will be ready in about a half an hour," Clint answered with a smile.

She narrowed her eyes at him, "You're being awfully nice to me all of a sudden, Hollywood."

He threw up a hand, and looked pained, "You wound me, angel! I'm always nice to you! In fact, after dinner, if you want I'll be extra nice to you and give you a full body massage."

Zoey laughed, but before she could respond, Tanner entered the room from the back door. He shocked her even further when she realized that he had a bottle of wine and a single red rose in his hands. Her mouth hung open, and his complexion darkened when their eyes met.

"Hey, Zoey. This is for you." He held out the rose, and she glanced at his brothers and then him in confusion.

"What is this for?"

Tanner looked to Clint and Dalton who both just smiled and left him to explain. "We wanted to do something nice for you tonight. You've been taking such great care of us all week…well…"

She took the rose from his hand, running her fingers over the soft petals and then down the stem. A thorn pricked the skin of her thumb and she hissed.

"Damn it. I knew I should have said yes when Roberta offered to de-thorn it," Tanner said, his jaw clenching. "Are you alright?"

"I'm fine. Thank you, the flower is beautiful exactly as it is, and thank you to you both too," she said, smiling at Clint and Dalton, "It means a lot to me that you guys would do this."

"Anything for you, angel," Clint said with a wink. "Better get that rose in water, and a Band Aid on that thumb. We can't have you bleeding out before dinner. Tanner, get the girl a glass of wine already. It's Friday night and she should be relaxing."

Tanner flipped Clint off, but he did as instructed, reaching up into the cabinet for a bud vase before he pulled out a wine glass. Zoey carefully removed the thorns and leaves from the long stem. The flower was perfect. Its deep crimson petals were wrapped in a full bud that would spread to become a stunning bloom. She felt a wave of warmth settle in her chest at the idea that Tanner Keegan had personally selected a flower for her. What a long ways they had come since that terrible night at Robin's so long ago.

When she finished with the flower, she turned to find all three men watching her, and she laughed. "What is it?"

Tanner's jaw clenched and he handed her a glass of wine, "Nothing. Why don't you go get off your feet until dinner. I need to go shower real quick. Dalton, did you call Ulysses about getting Devonshire's shoe replaced?"

Just like that, the moment was broken as Tanner and Dalton discussed a horse that had thrown a shoe that day. Clint gave her a wink, but he went back to working on the food prep, leaving her to do as she was told and head into the living room.

She sunk into the butter soft leather of the sofa, sighing with pleasure as she put the flower on the end table next to her, and took a sip of wine. Flavors exploded on her tongue, and the mellow scent of berry filled her nose. There was nothing of interest on TV so she stopped it on a music station, tapping her foot as Jason Derulo sang about "The Other Side".

Her eyes drifted shut, and she let herself be swallowed up in the lyrics of the song and the uplifting dance beat. She wondered if she could handle a fling with one of the three Keegan brothers. It wasn't like she would be here forever, in a couple of weeks Rachel's mom would go back to Oklahoma, and Zoey would be able to move in there if she hadn't found her own place yet. Living on the Triple T, she didn't have any rent to pay so she should be able to save up the money for a deposit pretty quickly. What if until then, she let herself be seduced by Clint, or even Dalton? There was no way she would offer herself up to any of them after being turned down so flatly by Tanner and then Dalton, but if she just flirted back a bit, maybe...

A sudden sinking of the sofa cushion next to her made her jump and her eyes flew open to find Clint settling in beside her.

"Whoa, sorry, angel. I didn't mean to scare you. I seem to have a particular talent for that." His arm went around the back of the couch just like Dalton's always seemed to do when he sat with her.

"It's alright, I guess I was lost in thought and didn't hear you come in." She reached for the remote and turned the volume down on the TV as Christina Aguilera started singing "Your Body".

"That's a good song," Clint said, stealing the remote from her hand to turn it up just as she sang about finishing off on her own. What a fitting song for the thoughts she had been having a moment ago. "You know, I got to meet her once."

"Who?"

"Christina. I guess meet isn't quite the right word. I got to park her car once when I was working as a valet."

Zoey laughed out loud, and Clint's eyes widened. "You have got to do that more often. You're beautiful when you laugh."

A snort slipped out and she shook her head. "And you are a Grade A flirt."

"Grade A, huh? You really think so? I'd rather be a Grade A prime piece of meat in your eyes, I think." He wiggled his eyebrows sending Zoey into another round of giggles. She whacked his shoulder with the back of her hand, and he grabbed it in both of his, holding it over his heart. "You're breaking my heart, angel. And here I thought we were going to get married and have a dozen kids together."

"A dozen? You have to be joking? I can't have a dozen kids, I would swell up to the size of a house!" she teased, and he tugged on her hand, pulling her against his chest.

"Perfect, as long as you're mine I don't care how big you are."

Clint swooped in for a kiss before she could respond, and she melted against him. Tomato sauce and man was all she tasted as his tongue swept past the barrier of her lips and stroked over her own. One of his hands slipped from between them to cup the back of her head, holding her in place for his mastery, and she lost herself in him.

Someone moaned, and then whimpered, and she was startled to realize it was her. Her hands flexed against his chest, fisting into the fabric of his t-shirt, and kneading the muscles of his pecks as she kissed him back.

A sharp slap on her raised ass broke them apart, and she turned to glare at Dalton, still breathing hard. "What the hell?"

"Save a little sugar for me, pretty lady. Clint here has to go check his masterpiece. The timer just went off." Dalton looked way too pleased to have come upon her making out with his little brother, and she couldn't decide if she was irritated or if she wanted to kiss him so she could compare the two.

Her lips tingled, and her pussy clenched when Clint brushed a sweet kiss over her mouth and then swaggered into the kitchen leaving her alone with Dalton. She turned a hard look on his grinning face.

"You enjoyed that."

He gave her an innocent look, "What? The interrupting part, or the part where I got to watch from the doorway as you tried to swallow Clint's tongue down your throat?"

Face flaming, Zoey glared at him with all of the intensity she could muster. It might have helped if he was wrong. "You know, a gentleman wouldn't point those things out."

Dalton's laugh boomed through the room, and she fought to keep a straight face, "Whatever gave you the idea that I was a gentleman, pretty lady?"

Zoey tipped her chin arrogantly, "I wasn't the one who put the brakes on."

His blue eyes flared with heat, and he stalked her. Slowly but surely he edged closer to where she sat on the sofa until he was close enough to reach out and pull her up against his chest. Her hands gripped his shoulders to keep from tumbling backwards, but she knew instinctively that if she let go he wouldn't let her fall. Two large hands reached down to squeeze her ass, his pinky fingers falling just below the hem of her shorts so they settled in the connecting crack where her upper thigh stopped and her ass curved.

"I won't ever make that mistake again, Zoey." Dalton's voice had dropped a couple of octaves so it was low and growly, and it skittered over her already aroused body like fingers. "Just give me the signal, and I'll have you naked and spread before you can take a breath."

Her lips parted on an exhale as his words slammed into her brain. This was what she wanted, right? She could allow herself to be seduced into a fling and not feel guilty about it because they were both adults. Dalton's head tipped and one eyebrow rose questioningly, but as she rose up on her toes for a kiss, Tanner walked back into the room.

"What is going on?" Tanner snapped harshly.

To her surprise, Dalton didn't let her go, instead he just shifted her to his side so he could turn to face his older brother. "Nothing now, but if you would have been a few minutes longer you might have gotten a show."

Clint's voice called out that supper was ready, breaking the tension, and thankfully both brothers let the conversation drop. Tanner stormed through the living room ahead of them, and Zoey looked up at Dalton warily.

"Don't worry, love, that's just a bit of jealousy. He hasn't had any competition for your affection until recently. He'll come around." Dalton gave her a gentle nudge and she led the way into the dining room.

Everyone took their seats silently and Clint gave them all a funny look. "Okay, what did I miss?"

"In a nutshell? You kissed Zoey, then I almost kissed Zoey, until Tanner interrupted and got jealous. Now she is second guessing herself, and I'm a little bummed that I didn't get my kiss in before he interrupted," Dalton said without even lifting his eyes from where he scooped lasagna onto his plate.

"You got your kiss last weekend," Zoey said petulantly, and then instantly regretted letting the words fall off her tongue. Tanner's jaw flexed, and Clint's eyes went wide.

"Wow. I didn't figure Dalton would be the first," Clint said with a shake of his head.

"He wasn't," Zoey whispered, staring at Tanner.

Now all eyes were on the oldest Keegan brother. Zoey wanted him to speak up, but he stayed stoically silent, leaving his brothers to their imagination. The deep crease between his eyebrows and the quick jump of the pulse in his throat signaled his discomfort, and Dalton and Clint turned to her for answers. Seeing their curiosity, Zoey shook her head and stared down at her food. Clint had taken her plate and served her the moment they took their seats, and per her normal request he had only given her half of what he and his brothers took, but even that looked enormous. Her mouth tasted like sawdust, and her stomach felt like it was full of lead.

It was clear to her that Tanner didn't want news of their kiss shared. Was he ashamed of her? What was the rose and wine for then? Suddenly she felt ridiculous. For just a moment, she thought that maybe all of this meant something. Her heart melted at the knowledge that these three men might genuinely care about her in some small way, and then Tanner had to go and fuck it up with that one look.

Shoving her chair back, she gave Clint a shaky smile, "Thank you, Clint, for cooking dinner tonight. I really appreciate it, but I've suddenly lost my appetite."

She didn't wait for a response. She just grabbed her wine glass, and made a beeline for her room. There was nothing more to say. Tanner wanted her, but only if he could have her in secret, and it killed her to think that he might be ashamed to be with her. Sure, she was the daughter of the town's biggest junkies, but she figured she had overcome the judging and horrific pitying assumptions.

After all, she had gone to college. She had gotten her goddamn master's degree for fuck's sake. Just who the hell did he think he was? She was absolutely good enough for him. In fact, she was too good for him. Her spine stiffened as she resolved to stop caring so much what Tanner thought. It seemed like she just continued to let him hurt her over and over again until she was nothing but a self-conscious mess.

Well, no more. She was done feeling sorry for herself, and letting someone make her feel less than adequate. If Tanner didn't see her worth, then perhaps Dalton or Clint would, and she couldn't wait to see his reaction when he realized she had made her choice.

Throwing herself on her bed and scooping up her book, she refused to let the tears fall for Tanner again. Too many times had she let him make her feel small. This time, she was going to overcome those doubts, no matter what.

An hour later she was engrossed in a BDSM story, and she had completely relaxed, letting go of her tension. Her heart lurched when someone knocked sharply on the bedroom door.

She hesitated a moment, and then set her book aside to answer it. To her surprise Tanner stood in the hallway with a plate full of food in one hand and her rose in the other.

"Tanner?"

His golden eyes looked wary, but he stood tall under her scrutiny. "I came bearing gifts, and an apology."

The reminder burned and she crossed her arms over her chest. "No thank you."

"Zoey, please. Let me come in for a minute and say my piece." She couldn't remember Tanner asking so sweetly for anything before, and indecision welled up in her chest. "I know I hurt you, but I didn't do it intentionally. I want a chance to make it right."

Pushing the door open, she stepped out of the way and let him into the bedroom. He put the plate and rose on the bedside table, and then took a seat on the bed. She saw him take note of her reading material and swallow hard. His whole body seemed to tense as he reached out and picked up her open book. Refusing to cower or be embarrassed of her choice in novels, she tried to assume an air of indifference as she took a seat next to him and retrieved it from his hands.

"You wanted to talk, so talk."

For just a moment, she saw heat in his eyes before he put it aside and reached for her hand. "I'm not ashamed of you, Zoey. I know that's what you thought, but it's not true. I'm ashamed that I took advantage of your situation."

"Took advantage—" Her temper flared, but Tanner pressed a finger to her lips stopping her from blowing up.

"You're in my house because you needed help. Not because you wanted to be accosted every waking minute. My temper got the best of me the other day, and when you asked me to kiss you, well, I didn't use good judgment. I had hoped that you would be able to put it aside and forgive me, but when you brought it up tonight I knew that I had hurt you."

Zoey stared at him in confusion. "You didn't want to kiss me? What was all of that crap in the truck about wanting to fuck me?"

For the first time ever Tanner's head dropped and he didn't look her in the eye. She tried to tell herself the uncomfortable twinge in her heart region was just a belly ache from lack of dinner, but the longer he was quiet, the more painful it got. Reaching out a hand, she placed it on his thick thigh in a silent attempt to encourage him. He stared down at it for a moment before he placed his big hand on top of hers and laced their fingers together.

"I'm not good enough for you, baby. As much as I want to be, it just can't happen that way." His voice was quieter than usual, and her mouth dropped open in shock.

"You're not good enough? *You're* not good enough? For me? Have you fallen off your horse recently, cowboy?" Caught between being confused, pissed, and elated, she struggled to find the right words. "Tanner Keegan, I have wanted you since I was a teenager. Back when I was skinny, pimply, and awkward. But every time I have offered, you have slapped me down. Now you're trying to get me to buy that it's because you honestly believe you aren't good enough? Who the fuck is going to be good enough for me, Tanner? Do you think I'm so shallow that I need a millionaire, or a movie star?"

"Hey, I'll be your movie star!" Clint's voice piped up, and Zoey fought to keep from grinning at him as he leaned against the door jam.

"I'm not a millionaire, but at least I wouldn't reject you, pretty lady."

Dalton appeared behind Clint, and Zoey rolled her eyes at the pair of them.

"Can't you two give us a few minutes of privacy?" Tanner snapped, glaring at his younger brothers.

Dalton shook his head, "Nope, not when it involves all of us, and someone we care about. We're all four going to have to talk it out if this relationship is going to work."

If Zoey hadn't already been sitting, she would have dropped to the floor in shock. "Relationship? What are you talking about?"

The two younger Keegan's moved into the room, Clint stood in front of her, while Dalton took a seat on the other side of the bed behind her. She stared up at Clint who took her free hand in his, she was surprised to realize that her other hand was still gripped by Tanner.

"They are just being assholes and trying to piss me off." Tanner's tone had changed, and she could tell he was really upset at the intrusion.

Clint shook his head, "No, we're trying to be honest about our intentions with the lady. Just because you're too chicken shit to admit you want her, doesn't mean we are. Angel, I know you and I are just getting to know each other, but—"

Zoey jerked her hands away from both of them, and stood up abruptly. "No."

"No?" Dalton said, while Clint just looked stunned. Tanner's eyes narrowed on her and he crossed those muscular arms over his big chest waiting for her to explain.

Taking a shaky breath, she moved farther away from the three of them. Did they even know what seeing them on her bed did to her? It was like all of the air had been sucked out of the room and she was feeling hot and slightly claustrophobic, so she began pacing. "What I mean is no, we're not having this conversation. I like you guys, and you already know what you do to me when you kiss me." She took a moment to make eye contact with all three of them. In their own ways they each looked masculinely smug. "But I won't be the cause of a divide in your family, and I won't settle for anyone who can't be honest about what he wants." This time she glared at Tanner pointedly. He had the decency to look a little ashamed, and she felt empowered.

"I'm only here for another week or two, so let's make the best of it and part as friends. No more pissing on my leg for each other's benefit because I'm no one's territory, got it?" She waited for each man's nod before she smiled, "Besides, just because it's temporary doesn't mean it won't be fun."

Clint's face spread into a wide grin, and Dalton's eyes took on a wicked glint. Tanner's previously smug and arrogant persona was gone, in its place was fury and contempt. "Are you saying you will fuck us, but you won't date us?"

"Tanner!"

"Fuck that man!"

Zoey stared him down silently while his two brothers blew up on him trying to protect her honor. When they had blown off their steam she stepped closer to where he stood next to the bed. "No. Years ago I offered my body to you, and you turned me down flat. I promised myself I would never do it again. This time if you want me, you will have to work for it, cowboy. So enjoy sitting on the sidelines watching your brothers have all of the fun." She paused for effect, and then pointed to the door. "Now, you can all leave. I'm tired and I want to go to sleep."

It was like the wall broke between them, and Tanner looked hurt as he stormed past her out of the bedroom without a word. Clint and Dalton exchanged a look.

"Zoey, it doesn't have to be like this," Dalton said softly, moving around the bed to stand on her right, while Clint moved to her left and ran his hand over her ponytail.

"Yes it does. I know you two think you know me, but you don't know everything yet, and when you do, well...the point is that right now all I have to offer you is something temporary. Trust me, once word gets around the three Keegan men are back in town and on the market, you will be glad." She let Dalton wrap her in his arms, pressing her face into his chest and inhaling deeply as she tried to control her emotions.

Clint moved in behind her and pressed a kiss to the side of her neck, giving her a gentle squeeze before she lifted her head again. "I disagree, angel, but I won't push you. Tonight you better get some sleep because you have a date tomorrow with two lonely cowboys."

She gave him a small smile, and accepted a sweet kiss from each of them before they left the room. Tears were running down her cheeks before she even managed to sink down onto the bed, and she grew irritated with herself. So much for not crying over Tanner ever again, this was turning into a routine.

Tanner Keegan wanted a woman who was a born rancher's wife, someone who would stay at home and take care of his children while stroking his ego. Zoey knew what her flaws were. With her tainted blood, and career driven future, she certainly didn't fit that bill. Her food grew cold on her plate, long forgotten as she cried herself to sleep yet again for the cowboy that didn't want her for keeps.

## CHAPTER EIGHT

Saturday dawned clear and warm, and Zoey allowed herself the luxury of sleeping in late. Of course, to anyone else eight-thirty a.m. wasn't late, but in her book that was wasting half the day. The house was quiet as she fixed herself coffee and toast. Her thoughts kept circling around the brothers and their conversation last night.

She had to be completely honest with herself, there was no way to make everyone happy, so it wasn't even worth trying. Instead, she would focus on enjoying the time she had with Clint and Dalton before she moved on. It wasn't like Stone River was a mecca of the dating world, it could be years before she had sex again, so that was at the top of her to do list with the Keegan men.

Knowing that all three of them desired her sexually put an extra bounce in her step as she dressed and headed out to the barn. For the first time in years she was going to embrace her inner seductress and enjoy it.

Clint was in the barn working when she stepped inside. She took a second to admire the snug fit of his jeans, and the broad sweep of his shoulders from afar. He had settled right back into the ranching life as if he never left, and it suited him.

"Morning, cowboy," she called out as she stepped over to pat a mare in the first stall.

His head came up and a wide grin split his face, deepening the cleft in his chin, and enhancing whatever it was that made him so damn attractive. "Morning, angel." He dropped the crate of tools he was holding to the floor, and made a beeline for her. Just before he reached her side, he paused to check out her backside in her favorite pair of jeans. "Damn, you are one sexy woman, Zoey Carson."

She cringed in her head when she heard herself giggle like a teenager. Did mature women planning to have an affair giggle at compliments?

"Thank you. What are you working on today?" she asked, feeling warmer when his hands found her hips and turned her into the cove of his body.

"Hmm? Oh, a little of this and a little of that, nothing so important that I can't leave it for now. How about a little romp in the hay?" His eyebrows wiggled, and she caught herself before she giggled again.

"I was thinking more about going for a ride."

Immediately she knew he had the wrong idea, but she enjoyed the way his face seemed to light up at the suggestion, so she didn't correct it. "Oh, baby, you're speaking my language now!" His head dipped as he kissed her breathless, pressing her back against the rough wood of the stall behind her.

It took every bit of inner will power to push him away and shake her head, "No, I don't mean riding a cowboy, I mean riding a horse. I haven't had a chance to refresh my skills, and I've been on the ranch for a week. Do you think Tanner would mind?"

Clint looked thoroughly dejected, "Am I so resistible that you would rather have a horse between your thighs than me?"

Zoey pressed a finger to his pouting lips. "Not a chance and you know it. However, I am not interested in a lecture from Tanner should he happen to catch us, and I am not a closet exhibitionist. I prefer my private life be private."

Clint's smile grew again, "Now that's an answer I'll accept, because ya didn't say no. Come on, we'll saddle up a couple of horses and explore the ranch together. Tanner has added some land to the Triple T that I haven't gotten to check out yet."

They were in the saddle in record time, and Zoey laughed along with

Clint as he pointed out various spots and told stories from when the three boys were young. A little smidge of her was envious of their fantastic childhood. She had always dreamed about having parents who were responsible enough that she could be childishly irresponsible. Instead of swinging from trees and tipping cows, she was making herself dinner and dodging the bill collectors' phone calls. In a quiet moment, Clint turned and looked at her carefully.

"How long have you been in love with Tanner?"

If she hadn't been holding the reins in her hands she might have fallen out of the saddle in shock. "What?"

"After you went to sleep last night Dalton and I talked for a while. We both know you're in love with Tanner, but we also know that you're attracted to the two of us. Is it too much to hope that you might be open to a ménage relationship long term?"

Zoey couldn't speak. She just gaped at him. Clint was the fun brother, not the serious one, but here he was asking her a very serious question. Forcing herself to continue breathing, she shrugged.

"Tanner and I have a history, yes. I'm not sure that I know what love is to be able to say I'm in love with him." She was startled to see a glimmer of fear in his tawny brown eyes when she looked over at him. "I don't know if a ménage relationship would work for the four of us. I really don't know you and Dalton that well yet. I can't say yes to it, but I won't say no either."

He gave her a reassuring wink, "That's all I can ask for, angel. Give us some time to show Tanner that this could work."

"Why are you so sure that it could? You've only been back in Texas for a week, and I don't think you've even been into town more than twice yet."

It was Clint's turn to shrug. "I once asked pops how he knew that mama was the right woman for him, and he told me sometimes you just know. They met at a church picnic, and mama was already going steady with another guy. Pops says it was love at first sight for him and he wasn't about to let her go without a fight. It took him six months to convince her he was serious about her, and four years of asking to get her to marry him."

"Wow! Most people would have given up after four years."

"What's a few years when you have a lifetime ahead of you? Angel, I'm nothing but a broke down man who couldn't make it as an actor. Just knowing you'll consider me, makes me the happiest I've been in years."

Zoey glanced at him warily to see if he was joking, but his expression remained serious. "I'm not sure I'm worthy of such adoration, Clint. I'm not exactly Miss America, and the only stories I can tell from my childhood are ones that involve mom getting high in the living room while I tried to study, or sleep. I never even knew where my dad was most of the time. Seems to me that trying to reach for your dreams, and failing, is a whole lot better than never trying."

Clint stopped his horse, and his brown eyes bored into hers searching her gaze for something. "Angel, you couldn't have uttered a more perfect phrase. I knew you were perfect for me."

"Ha! You're just getting to know me. Trust me, I'm not always an angel."

A wicked glint appeared in his eyes as he laughed, "Good. I can't wait to see you let the devil loose. I bet she's a lot of fun."

Zoey laughed with him, and brushed off his sensual teasing. "There are so many things about me that you guys don't know yet."

He observed her silently for a few moments, all hint of laughter gone from his eyes. "I remember you from when we were kids. I might have been five years older than you, but Stone River is a small place. Everyone knew about your family situation."

She grimaced and then huffed, "Yep, everyone knew, and yet no one did anything to help me."

"I wish I could have helped you back then. I remember seeing you walking home one day in the dead of winter without a coat and thinking you were a silly girl. I said something to my mama as we drove home, and she scolded me. She explained to me that not everyone had the same luxuries that I did, and fed me a heaping helping of humble pie."

Zoey's throat tightened, "You! You and your mama gave me that green coat didn't you?"

Clint's cheeks grew ruddy when he realized that he had given up his secret, and he had trouble meeting her eyes. "We went that night and bought it. Left for school thirty minutes early to make sure it was there for you to find."

Zoey could remember that moment as if it was yesterday. It was late November and the weather had just turned seriously cold. She had outgrown her previous coat by a couple of years and it was so frayed and tattered it did her no good anyway. Each morning she spent twenty minutes trying to get just the right about of layers in order to avoid freezing to death on the two mile walk to school. One morning, as she walked out the front door with her books in hand, she was stunned to find a winter coat hanging on a tree limb in her front yard. It was hunter green and a small white tag hung from it like a price tag. Instead of an amount, it simply read, "For: Zoey." Until this moment she had never known where it came from.

Biting back a swell of emotion, she smiled at him, "Thank you."

He shrugged and winked back. A wealth of unspoken words passed between them, and Zoey barely managed to keep her tears in check. The whole way back to the ranch she held an inner battle with herself over whether or not she had led him on. It wasn't as if she was super experienced at juggling multiple men, and in this case, she wasn't even sure if she had two or three on the hook. But the more time she spent with him and his brothers, the more she learned about them, and the deeper her attachment grew to all three of them. How hard was it going to be to give them each equal pieces of herself, without losing her heart?

By the time they arrived back at the barn, it was lunchtime and the temperature had risen dramatically. Clint took her mare from her to unsaddle and she gratefully smiled and headed for the air-conditioned house.

A deep voice stopped her halfway up the porch steps, and she turned to find Tanner coming around the corner of the porch.

"Nice ride?"

"Yes, actually. I haven't been on a horse for a long time, and it was great to see more of the ranch. You boys are so lucky to have such a beautiful place to call home."

Tanner nodded, "Did he take you to see the glowing tree?"

"The what?"

"I guess that answers my question. It's a special place on the ranch, but he might have forgotten about it. It's been a decade since he was there. If you want I'll show you sometime."

Zoey stood there in shock. Was this the same man who left her bedroom pissed off last night? When he frowned at her hesitation, she nodded, "Yes, I would love to see it."

His wide shoulders seemed to relax and he gave her a half smile. "I better let you get inside to cool off." His eyes skimmed down her body taking in the sweaty t-shirt that clung to her breasts, and her skin tight jeans. Even from six feet away her skin tingled as if he had touched her.

When she couldn't make her tongue function to speak, she just turned on her heel and bolted into the house, leaving him standing on the porch. She went about the motions of showering and changing, but no amount of cold water seemed to reduce the burning in her body. Hopefully tonight's date would culminate in something more touchy feely than the horseback ride had.

Zoey managed to entertain herself for the rest of the day and didn't see any of the three Keegan brothers until almost dinnertime. She was just about to search the cabinets for dinner supplies when she heard Dalton and Clint on the front porch.

The two brothers came into the living room, and her mouth went dry. They were both shirtless, bareheaded, and carrying their boots in their hands. Their jeans were soaking wet, with muddy hems, and they were laughing like hyenas.

"What on God's green earth happened to you two?" she asked, planting her fists on her hips as she stared at the mess they were creating on the floor.

Clint snorted and looked to Dalton who just shrugged, "Attacked by the horse trough."

Zoey nodded, struggling to hold back a laugh. "And I take it the trough won?"

"Something like that," Dalton answered with a laugh "We're going to get cleaned up and then we can start our date, pretty lady."

She waved him off, "No big deal guys, I can cook—"

"NO!" the two men barked it out in unison, and Zoey took a step backwards.

Clint cleared his throat, "What we mean is, no please don't cook. We have the whole evening planned already."

"Oh, okay," she hesitated, feeling giddy with excitement that they planned something for her, and a little awkward because she really didn't like to be surprised, "Should I change?"

A quick glance down reminded her that she was wearing a pair of yoga pants and an oversized t-shirt. Her toes were bare, because she had just painted the nails a pretty pale pink color, and she wiggled them a little.

"Only if you want to. We're not going anywhere fancy this time. We want you to be comfortable," Dalton said.

She gave him a smile, and he crooked his finger at her. When she shook her head, he huffed, "Zoey, come here. I won't bite...unless you ask me to."

A shiver skittered down her spine and directly to her clit and she almost moaned out loud. She wanted to scream "Yes" and jump him right there. He was already half undressed, so it wouldn't take much to get her hands on the hard cock that pressed against his zipper. Finding her backbone, she walked across the room slowly until she stood just a foot or so away from them.

"And what if I want you to bite, cowboy?" Her nipples were throbbing against her t-shirt and she squeezed her thighs together to ease the pressure on her pussy.

Dalton groaned and grabbed her chin so she was forced to look him in the eye. "I really hope you do, but once I start I won't be able to stop, so unless you plan on showering with me, you better just stick with a kiss."

Zoey felt empowered to know that she had such an effect on him, and instead of a chaste kiss on his lips, she planted her hands on his bare chest and nipped his bottom lip. "I'll skip the shower for now, but later..."

Dalton wasted no time. His fingers tangled into her long black hair, and he held her still so he could ravage her mouth. Seducing and overpowering her with a kiss. When he finally pulled away she was lying limply against his chest, and moisture had seeped through her clothing to her skin.

Clint tugged on her wrist, and Dalton released her reluctantly into his brother's arms. "Since you're already wet…"

Zoey moaned loudly just before Clint's mouth descended on hers. He had to have known how she would take his statement, and she had no doubt the two of them knew what they were doing to her body.

When Clint broke the kiss Zoey's brain was barely computing, and she remained pressed against his muscular chest, reeling from her own desire. "Damn you boys can kiss," she muttered, and both men laughed loudly.

Dalton tugged her hair sharply as he walked past her toward the stairs to his room. "We can do more than that, pretty lady, but you have to wait until tonight for more. Come on, Clint."

Clint gave her a smack on the ass before making sure she was steady on her feet and heading down the hall to the bathroom. She stared after him as her heart settled back into a normal rhythm. If a kiss was so explosive between them, sex was going to be nuclear. Smiling to herself, she went to change clothes for the second time that day.

---

"What the hell is that for?" Dalton watched as Clint added a bottle of wine to the backpack he was supposed to have filled with food. They had a detailed plan for their date tonight with Zoey, but it didn't include getting her drunk.

"Spin the bottle, duh?" Clint winked at him, but Dalton could feel his face pinch in a frown. It was important this date go perfectly if they wanted to convince Zoey that they were serious about her. She seemed determined to keep them at arm's length and stay in control. Dalton was equally determined to shake her up. "I figured it wouldn't hurt to have it with us in case it gets chilly up there tonight. I'll put it back if it's that big of a deal."

Dalton shook his head, "No, keep it. You're right, she might like a drink later. I just don't want her to think we're trying to get her liquored up, so we can then fuck her."

Clint's eyes widened, "Dude, you might not be trying to fuck her, but I sure as hell am. That's why I have lube and condoms in here too."

"I'm not saying that I don't want to fuck her, God, really? I'm saying this date is supposed to be about getting to know each other, not just getting her naked." Dalton finished packing the pile of gear into the back of his old Suburban, and frowned at Clint. "If we want her for longer than a couple of weeks, we have to give her time to adjust to the idea."

"I know, I mean, I do want her to want to stay, but I do my best convincing when I'm naked. I can't help it if I want to show her my best," said Clint.

Dalton was just about to tell Clint he couldn't go with them, when the front door creaked open, and both men turned to see a smiling Zoey headed their way. Her long hair was in a ponytail and Dalton made a mental note to relieve her of the restricting binding as soon as possible.

"Hey, guys, here is my bag. You aren't taking me over the border are you? Because my passport isn't up to date." Her smile was brighter than any star he'd ever seen, and he reached for her as she drew close.

Pulling her against his chest, he pressed a kiss to her forehead, "No, pretty lady, we aren't kidnapping you."

She rose up on her toes to peek around him at the gear and laughed, "Camping? We're going camping?"

"What's wrong with camping?" Clint asked, moving up against her back and kissing her shoulder.

"Oh, uh, nothing is wrong with it. I haven't been since I was a girl scout. I think I was about seven. I hope you two know what you're doing with that tent because otherwise we would be smarter to make a run for the border." When she laughed it filled his chest with a sweet warmth that he hadn't experienced before.

"Nope, no Mexican rice for you tonight, just hotdogs and s'mores over a campfire."

Her excitement was contagious as she bounced on her toes between them and laughed. "What are we waiting for? There is a marshmallow with my name on it so let's get going!"

The ride up to the bluffs that lined the northern edge of the Triple T took about a half an hour. Zoey seemed anxious to learn everything about them, and Dalton took that as a good sign. After exchanging favorite colors, foods, drinks, vacation destinations, books, and music, they still didn't seem to have any trouble finding things to talk about. It was the most comfortable he had ever been with a woman, and he felt more confident that their plan would work.

A lengthy phone call to Sawyer Brooks this morning had given him a few ideas on how to woo Zoey over to their way of thinking, and as much as he hated to let Clint have his way, sex was at the top of that list. The Brooks brothers had used seduction to land Rachel, and according to Sawyer, they had invested significant time both as a group and alone with her until she realized her own feelings.

As they pulled to a stop at the end of the working road, Zoey glanced around with a frown. "Where are we? All I see is trees. Is this still the Triple T?"

"Yep. We're going to the top of the bluffs that overlook the Cuyato River, it's the northern boundary of the ranch, and there is a great view of the sunset where we camp," Clint answered as Dalton went around to the back and started unloading their supplies.

Handing Zoey a backpack and a small cooler, he winked, "We have to hoof it from here, but it's not a long walk. Clint, grab the tent and take the lead."

As they followed the well-worn but slightly overgrown footpath, Dalton explained their choice of destination. "When we were kids the three of us boys would come up here and camp a lot. Mama and pops didn't worry about us up here because we were still on Triple T ground. We told ghost stories, built forts, and tree houses, snuck our first dirty magazines and our first drinks—"

"We even learned some first aid while we were up here," Clint added, and Zoey snorted.

"I can only imagine what kind of trouble the three of you got into all alone. How long has it been since you've been up here?" Dalton heard Zoey's question, but his eyes were focused on her curvy ass, so he had difficulty doing the math. For once Clint came to his rescue.

"The night I turned eighteen, me and some of my friends came up here to camp. The last time Dalton and Tanner came with me I think was Tanner's eighteenth birthday. Kinda makes me wish he would have joined us tonight."

Clint's words were like a kick in Dalton's gut. Without Tanner, it certainly felt weird. It was like the third leg of their stool was missing and they were swaying back and forth on just two legs, hoping they didn't topple. Could Zoey accept just the two of them if Tanner never came around?

Before Dalton could come up with an answer they had reached the clearing at the top of the bluff, and Zoey gasped. The view was pretty incredible. The other side of the river was land that used to belong to the Raft family but had recently become part of Brooks Pastures. It was prime grazing land, but the Brooks family raised horses in their own fields and had yet to start using it. As far as the eye could see there was tall green grass and blue sky.

"I have to admit, I'm impressed. I had no idea a place like this existed." Zoey stood at sharp edge of the bluff looking down into the rolling grayish green water of the river. "Has anyone ever fallen?"

Dalton felt his face drain of blood, and his knees wobble at her question. When she looked up at him her eyes widened in horror.

"Oh my God! I can't believe...I'm so sorry, Dalton! I didn't mean to ask that, or say that, or bring up bad things. Shit!" She rushed to his side, her hands skimming up his arms to cup his face. "Hey, look at me."

He focused on her eyes, and all he saw was deep concern there. Concern for him and his feelings. For over a decade he had been the one concerned about everyone else. In medical school he was concerned about his studies, his teachers, his classmates, but never himself. In Africa, he was a doctor, so it was his duty to be concerned about those around him. He was known to be selfless and unequivocally reliable. All of his life he had been the peacemaker between bossy Tanner, and bratty Clint, never concerned with what *he* wanted, only concerned with building a strategic compromise between the two sides. For the first time, he stared into the eyes of someone who was concerned for him and him alone.

His heart rocked in his chest, and he let out a deep breath before molding his body to hers. When he slammed his mouth down on hers, she didn't struggle or fight back, she just relaxed into him, submitting to his need for comfort. It was the perfect reaction, and his body agreed as lust slammed through him.

Digging his hands into her ass, he lifted her off the ground and she locked her ankles behind his hips as if she did it all the time. God, what he would give to feel her do this every day for the rest of his life.

"What the fuck, Professor? I thought you said we were supposed to hold off on the fucking!" Clint's voice registered, but Dalton couldn't have stopped himself at that point for anyone but Zoey, and she wasn't telling him to slow down.

In fact, she was digging her fingernails into his shoulders and sucking on his tongue like she was starving. The scent of her arousal was growing thick even though they were both fully clothed. Dalton forced himself to break their kiss long enough to breathe and ask, "Zoey, please say you're sure?"

"I'm sure. I thought I could wait, but I can't." Her lips nibbled at his jaw, and he groaned when she licked his earlobe.

"Fuck! Clint, grab the sleeping bags." Dalton dropped to his knees with Zoey still in his arms, and rested her weight on his thighs, "And the condoms!"

"I'm on it, Professor, just don't pop your cork until I'm back." Clint took off at a dead run to collect the last of their gear because it contained the two requested items.

Dalton stared down at Zoey. Her gorgeous blue eyes were dark with desire, and her lips were slightly swollen after he had savagely kissed her. Reaching up, he tugged the elastic band from her hair, and both of them sighed with pleasure as the glorious black satin tumbled down her back and into his hands.

"I like your hair down, kitten," he murmured as he pressed butterfly kisses all over the planes of her face, and stroked his fingers through her hair.

"Kitten?"

"Oh yeah. Trust me, in a few more minutes you'll be purring."

They were feasting on each other's mouths again when Clint reappeared, running at top speed. He had to have nearly flown to the truck and back, but Dalton was damn glad to see him.

Zoey climbed from his lap to help spread out the sleeping bags in a nice soft pallet, and slip her shoes and socks off. Dalton glanced at Clint who was still panting a bit from his run, and they both waited hesitantly for her to make the first move.

With a flirty smile, she turned so her back was to both of them, and standing in the center of the homemade love nest, she slowly slid the hem of her t-shirt up and over her head. Dalton's mouth went dry as dust, and all she had bared was the curve of her spine and her bra strap. When she began peeling her snug jeans from her hips and sliding them over her sexy legs he nearly dropped to his knees to grovel at her feet. Just as he suspected, her ass was lush and perfect, especially with the slim string of a thong splitting it in two.

"Oh hell, angel, you had to wear the sexy panties too?" Clint's groan echoed the one in Dalton's head, then she laughed and stepped from her jeans, pushing them to the side. Her fingers played with the clasp of her bra for barely a second before it too dropped to the ground.

That was the last straw for Clint. Dalton stood quietly as his little brother walked slowly around the spread of blankets to stand in front of their woman. Zoey's head tilted up and Dalton imagined she had that challenging jut of her chin going on she used so often.

"How does she look, Hollywood?" he asked softly as he began removing his own clothing as quickly as possible.

Clint's voice was low, and breathless. "Like an angel."

Zoey's gasp rocketed through Dalton's loins making his cock throb. He pressed himself against her back, and because of their height difference, it placed his cock at the top swell of her ass. Sliding his hands around, he cupped the two grapefruit sized tits that he had been dreaming about nightly, and sighed against her ear.

"Feels like one too."

"Mmm...that feels good," she moaned, leaning back into him with complete trust. His ego swelled along with his dick as she wriggled against him.

Her moaning stopped when Clint finally moved in to kiss her, and Dalton flinched when he felt Clint's hands come around her body to her back. He had to take a little step back because it seemed a little weird to be touching his brother at the same time as touching Zoey. This was going to take some getting used to. Continuing to pinch her nipples, and squeeze her tits, while avoiding Clint's roaming hands, grew trickier, and he finally huffed. "Let's lay her down."

Once Zoey was on her back, Dalton felt a lot more comfortable with the arrangement. Clint took over where he had been, sucking one plump pink nipple into his mouth, and squeezing the other. Touching was weird, but watching his brother with Zoey was fucking hot. She arched up off the bedding, her back a curve of passion as she clutched Clint's head to her chest, and encouraged him with moans and whimpers of pleasure.

Her legs were slightly spread, showing off a dripping wet pussy topped by a neatly trimmed triangle of dark curls. He could tell she was extremely aroused, because her clit was poking out from between her labia as though it was begging for his attention. Using his shoulders, to spread her thighs wider, he settled in for a closer look at her sweet cunt.

Just like her ass, her pussy lips were plump and perfect, and she cried out when he ran his finger through her juices and then pressed into her tight passage. She was tight as a virgin, and his balls drew up underneath him burning with need. Counting in his head for distraction from his nuts, he began circling his tongue around her swollen clit. He avoided too much pressure on the little nub so she didn't come too fast. He wanted her to remember the moment she had her first orgasm with the two of them for the rest of her life.

She was dripping wet, and thrusting her hips hard enough to jar him from his mission. When her hands began pressing on his head, he stopped long enough to capture them, holding them under her hips while he continued to feast on her pussy.

Clint rose up next to her head on his knees and ran his cock over her face, momentarily distracting Dalton yet again. Fuck, she looked seriously hot with a cock in her mouth. Her lush lips spread, and her tiny pink tongue darted out to capture the pre-cum that was on the head.

After a few thrusts to stretch her lips, Clint was able to slide into her mouth and from his angle, Dalton could see the lump that expanded the top part of her throat proving how deep she held him. It was all he could do not to come all over the sleeping bag, as he rose to his knees, and sheathed his cock in a condom.

"I can't wait, kitten. I need to be inside of you."

Clint slid back, giving Zoey some room to breathe as Dalton pushed the fat head of his cock into her snug opening. It took multiple thrusts before his balls were slapping her ass, but the sensation brought stars to his eyes. With his cock securely buried in the tightest pussy he had ever experienced, and his vision filled with his woman's mouth full of dick, he fucked her.

Every ounce of the emotions he had been battling and trying to contain swamped him, and poured into his actions. Zoey's hands held onto Clint's cock now, and her ankles rested on Dalton's shoulders. She was sexier than any porn star Dalton had ever seen, with her skin covered in a sheen of sweat and her breasts bouncing. He couldn't hold back any longer when she began spasming around his dick. He heard her choke just before Clint pulled his cock from her mouth and came all over her beautiful breasts, and then his vision grayed as cum shot from his balls and poured out of his dick into the condom.

---

Zoey's brain was spinning and she was fighting to fill her lungs. Dalton laid slumped half on and half off her with his now slightly softer cock still buried balls deep inside of her. Clint rested on his haunches looking as though he had just been through twelve rounds with a professional boxer. Zoey could relate to that. Her body sizzled as waves of bliss washed over her from head to toe, and her own cream dripped out of her.

So this was what being with two men was like. It was better than good, it was fan-fucking-tastic. In fact, as soon as she caught her breath, she wanted to give Clint a chance to match his big brother, or at least give him the ride of his life.

"Are you alright, pretty lady?" Dalton asked, reaching his hand out to brush her hair away from her face. "We weren't exactly gentle."

She gave him a half smile, "And I greatly appreciate that. I won't break. I'm not a china doll."

"Thank God," Clint murmured before pressing a sweet kiss to her mouth. "I never did like slow and sweet. If I'm going for a ride, I want it to be hard, fast, and steal my breath."

Zoey felt her smile widen as he used his discarded t-shirt to clean off her breasts. "I'm glad you feel that way, cowboy because as soon as you've recovered, I plan on saddling up."

Clint's eyes went wide, and then he barked out a loud laugh. "You. Are. Fucking. Perfect." When he kissed her this time it wasn't sweet, it was soul stealing. His tongue lashed at hers, and his teeth nipped her lips. The fire that had heated her blood slowly grew again, and she reached out to pinch his nipple in retaliation.

Dalton moved off her, allowing her to roll over onto her knees, and she shoved at Clint's shoulders. "Lay down, Hollywood."

"Bossy woman. You think you can handle me?" Clint threw back as he did what she instructed.

"I can handle you, *and* your brother." Zoey picked up a condom from where they had been dropped, and she covered Clint's growing erection with minimal fumbling. If it weren't for the remaining stickiness on her breasts, she might have wondered if he had really orgasmed just moments before. In fact, Dalton was now stroking his semi-hard cock and he would be ready to go again in another moment. Pleased with the stamina both brothers had, she quickly pressed her wet slit down over Clint's cock, bracing herself with her hands on the center of his chest, and wiggling until he filled her completely.

"Yeah, baby, take it all. Now fuck me." Clint's dirty talk did wicked things to Zoey's brain and body, and she began an easy rocking motion that allowed her to grind her clit on his pubic bone while beckoning for Dalton to come closer.

She hadn't given all that many blow jobs in her life, and she had never once enjoyed one, but something about the awe and adoration on their faces made her chest puff up with pride. Knowing both men enjoyed what she did, helped make it more enjoyable for her, and she relaxed her jaw allowing Dalton to slide in past her tonsils. As with Clint, it took a couple of tries, and it was slightly more awkward while trying to maintain a steady thrusting movement, but she managed to get into a rhythm.

When the first ripples of orgasm started and her motions faltered, they took over. Dalton's hand went to her head, holding her in place while he fucked into her mouth. His thrusts were shorter so she wasn't trying to focus on deep throating, and she was able to focus on the sensations in her body. Clint gripped her hips and began thrusting up to meet her, ensuring that she still got the hard contact on her clit she needed in order to fall over the cliff of climax.

She screamed around Dalton's cock, feeling her own saliva and his semen running off her lips. Trying not to think about how it looked, she focused in on the two brothers nearly simultaneous groans of completion. If this was what a ménage was like, then she could understand why Rachel walked around with such a contented cat smile on her face all the time.

For the first time in her life, she let someone take over and take care of her. After a few minutes of recovery cuddling, the two men went to work cleaning her up and setting up camp for the night. They redressed for comfort more than modesty, and then spent the rest of the evening sharing ghost stories, roasting hot dogs and marshmallows, and just being blissfully happy with their company.

If there was one dark spot to their happy moment, it was that Tanner wasn't with them. The knowledge tickled at the back of her brain, as did the realization that she was kidding herself if she thought she could give this up and walk away from them.

By the time they had made love again, and were slipping off into sleep in the sleeping bags, Zoey was determined to convince Tanner that she was the woman for him. Somehow she would find a way to prove to him that she was good enough, even with a shitty past because she knew she would never truly be happy without all three Keegan men in her life.

## CHAPTER NINE

It hurt to watch Zoey leave with Dalton and Clint, but it hurt even more when they all came back on Sunday morning looking freshly fucked and satisfied. Tanner's balls were bluer than the sky even though he had jerked off at least three dozen times in the week Zoey had lived on the Triple T.

He watched her easily step into an affectionate lover role with his brothers, and his heart ached to have her reach for him too. What he wouldn't give to kiss her before he walked out the door each morning, a promise for the night to come. Instead, he started avoiding her more and more as he fought to control his blinding desire.

Sure it made sense that she would want Clint and Dalton. One had movie star looks and charm to back them up, while the other had a promising career as a doctor ahead of him and the ability to give her the security she never had as a girl. What did he have for her? A ranch that fought to stay profitable, and his six day work week from sun up to sun down with barely any time for her. No. He was absolutely not what was best for Zoey Carson. Even if he wanted her with every ounce of his being.

"Hey, Skipper, how's it hanging?" Clint asked as he helped Zoey from the truck and carried a load of stuff into the house.

Tanner's eyes were on Zoey, watching her every hypnotic movement as though his next breath depended on it. *Get it together, man, she just slept with your brothers.* Instead of cooling his ardor, the mental images his thoughts inspired just made his cock throb.

"Hey, Tanner," she said softly, moving to stand directly in front of him. He had to fist his hands to keep from reaching out to touch her.

"Hey, Zoey, how was camping? Did they feed you enough?"

She laughed, "Oh yeah, I can't say I've ever had a better tasting marshmallow. The bluff was beautiful, and the view of the sunset was...breathtaking."

Tanner nodded politely as he shifted on his feet. Did she mean for her eyes to get all dreamy and her soft lips to part seductively? "I'm glad you had a good time. I have to go into town later for a few things, did you want to ride along?"

"Yes, that would be great. I think Dalton is wanting to talk to Doc Plass, so he might want to come along, is that alright?" She looked up at him with those big blue eyes and he nodded immediately.

*Damn it. I'm supposed to be the one in control with women. How does this little drop of a woman manage to keep directing me?* Feeling a surge of irritation, he stepped backwards and turned away from her deliberately. "I want to be back before sunset, so we'll leave by noon."

Without turning back for a response, he headed for the barn. Sunday was his day off from the ranch, but today he didn't feel like relaxing in his own house. Instead, he would work so hard that he would forget to think about Zoey, and her whisker burned throat, or the missing buttons on Clint's shirt. He would find a way to live with the hand he was dealt, somehow.

---

The ride to town was filled with quiet tension. Tanner was giving both Zoey and Dalton the cold shoulder, and it was making things awkward. A big part of her wanted to just flip out on him and ask him what the hell his problem was, but in her gut, she knew she wasn't ready to hear his answer. If he rejected her again, she wasn't sure she could survive it.

Instead, she bit her tongue and acted like she wasn't affected. Dalton was fidgeting on the seat next to her, and she finally reached out to lace her fingers through his. The gratitude in his blue eyes relaxed her a little. Here she was worrying about what Tanner thought when Dalton was getting ready to face his worst fears. Walking back into Stone River and possibly coming face to face with Walt or Minnie White.

"It will be alright," she murmured. A small thrill went through her when he pressed a soft kiss to her temple and stroked his thumb over her palm.

"I know, how could it not be when I have you with me?"

Tanner snorted, and Zoey shot him an icy glare. When he pointedly ignored her, she huffed, "Well I doubt they will even be in town. It's Sunday after all, surely there is a football game on or something."

That made both men laugh. "You're probably right, kitten. It's just a lot to take in. I never thought I would be doing this," Dalton swallowed hard.

"Doing what? Going to the Merc?" Tanner said with a snarky tone.

"Shut up, Skipper. You know what I mean."

Zoey squeezed Dalton's hand, "Things are different now. You're not a little kid anymore, and surely they wouldn't still be angry at you. You didn't do anything wrong."

"She's right, Professor. Walt and Minnie wouldn't want you to keep running," Tanner said, surprising them both. He looked up at their shocked faces, "What? I don't always agree with her, but this time she's absolutely correct. You've taken on a mountain of guilt you never had a right to own. It's not fair to you, it's not fair to the White's, and it isn't fair to Ben's memory."

Zoey wanted to throw her arms around Tanner and kiss him for his words. They seemed to bring an entirely new light into Dalton's eyes and his shoulders lifted again.

"Thanks for that," Dalton gave Tanner a half smile, and the silence resumed in the truck leaving them all to their own thoughts.

By the time they arrived, Zoey was determined to find a way to bring Dalton and the White's together. Her heart told her that Dalton had seen the situation through the eyes of a child, and he misinterpreted their feelings. If she could find a way to get him to talk to them, she just knew it would help him over his fear of remaining in Stone River. And if he stayed, well, that just opened all sorts of doors that seemed locked up tight before.

Tanner exited the truck and headed down the sidewalk toward the opposite end of town without a word, leaving Zoey and Dalton.

"I need to stop in and talk to Doc, will you be alright shopping alone?" Dalton asked as he helped her out of Tanner's pickup.

She snickered, "Uh yeah, I've only been doing my own grocery shopping since I was eleven. I think I can manage."

His fingers brushed back a piece of her long dark hair that had escaped from her ponytail. "Don't be like that. I only asked because I don't know if I will be alright alone. I miss you when we're apart, believe it or not."

Zoey felt a wave of warmth wash over her, and she melted. Accepting his kiss, she watched him walk across the street and into Thomas Plass's office. Hopefully their meeting would be a good one. Doc Plass was in his early seventies and after his wife passed away two summers ago, he had been looking for a way to retire. Dalton might be the solution he needed.

Forcing her feet to move, Zoey went into the Merc and got to shopping. By the time she made her way up to the register she had her cart laden with groceries and she was feeling exhausted. The sleepless night filled with aerobic activity had zapped all of her energy, and she was in dire need of a nap.

Hal McCrite was waiting near the register as she started to unload her cart. Ignoring the cashier, he jumped right in and started to bag things as they were checked out. "So, you're living with all three of the Keegan boys now, huh?"

Zoey didn't even bother to look up. "I'm still living on the Triple T. If that's what you're asking."

"And all three of them live there too?" Hal continued, and Zoey gave a sharp nod. "So does that mean wedding bells might be—"

"What it means is, that you need to mind your own business, McCrite. Unless you want to lose all of the Triple T's business."

Zoey jumped at Tanner's voice. The angry look on his face was clear enough, and Hal stuttered an apology quickly finding something more pressing to do. Before Zoey could offer up her debit card, Tanner had his wallet out and was paying the grocery bill. The young cashier looked up at him with a smitten glow in her eyes Zoey found particularly revolting, but she kept her mouth shut.

The moment they were back at the truck, she thanked him.

"For what?" Tanner asked, looking puzzled.

"For putting Hal in his place back there. You didn't have to say anything, but it means a lot to me that you did." She gave him a small smile while handing him another bag.

Tanner froze, "I would never let anyone say something shitty about you, Zoey, and that includes insinuating that you're fucking around."

"But I am, aren't I? Fucking around?" She tried to hold his gaze, but ultimately her eyes dropped to stare at the tiny dark hairs that were peeking above the open collar of his shirt.

"Are you? Because I thought you might really have feelings for my brothers," Tanner said softly. His fingers came up under her chin, forcing her to meet his eyes. "Until you say differently, you are still under my protection."

Again she experienced an oddly warm feeling from her belly to her clit as she stared up into his gold eyes. Did he know what that did to her? The fire that smoldered in his gaze answered her unspoken question, and she inhaled sharply.

Before she could say anything, he released her and resumed loading the groceries into the bed of the pickup. She watched as he carefully arranged everything cold into the two coolers they had brought specifically for transporting, and closed all of the other bags into the long silver toolbox that stretched under the back window. He was always so meticulous and careful in everything he did. It both amazed and bewildered her. The one thing he seemed unsure of was her.

A jolt of surprise shot down her spine. Tanner still wanted her. He wanted her in a very non-friend way, and it thrilled her to realize it. A plan was just beginning to form in her brain when Dalton walked up. His arms came around her, and he pressed a kiss to the crown of her head.

"All done?"

Smiling up at him she nodded, "Yep, Tanner was just helping me load it up. How about you? How did it go with Doc?"

"You are looking at Stone River's new family physician, well, so long as I accept the job that is. Doc Plass has been having more and more trouble with his arthritis, and he has decided to move to Tallahassee, Florida, to live with his daughter and her family. Finding a new doctor to take over a small town practice is about as hard as you can imagine, so he was elated to hear that I was back." Dalton was watching his older brother as he answered.

Tanner was quiet for a moment before he smiled at them both, "Congratulations, Doctor Keegan, and welcome home."

The two brothers shook hands and then hugged while laughing.

"This calls for a celebration before we go home!" Tanner said, giving Zoey a wink, "Robin's is closed, so I can't buy you a drink, Professor, but I can get you a cone from the Ice Cream Shoppe if you're game?"

Dalton looked over at her, and she nodded, "Oh yeah, I think a cone with one scoop of chocolate mountain and one scoop of peppermint sounds perfect!"

"Well then lead the way, m'lady!" Dalton bowed elegantly gesturing that Zoey go ahead of him, and she did so laughing all the way down the street to the shop.

Dottie was behind the counter as always, her light gray hair with a soft blue tint was pulled up into her own unique version of a bouffant, and her green eyes were lined with blue eyeliner and eye shadow that gave her a particularly disturbing wide awake look. For all her makeup skills were lacking, her sweet genuine personality made up for it, and she greeted the three of them as they filed through the door.

"Zoey Carson, where you been girl?" She gave them all a once over and then her penciled eyebrow rose, "Hmm....guess you found better things to do, huh?"

"Miss Dottie, we are celebrating today, so we need three cones—two scoops each, as well as a small container of Butter Pecan to take home to Clint," Tanner said, turning his most charming smile on the older woman.

"Whoa, two scoops? What's the occasion?" Dottie asked as she pulled out three large waffle cones.

"New beginnings," Dalton piped up, exchanging a glance with Zoey, and then waiting for Tanner's nod of agreement.

"I'd say that's a great thing to celebrate. By the way, welcome home Doctor Keegan." Dottie put the emphasis on the doctor title, and Dalton flushed a little.

"It's still Dalton for you, Miss Dottie."

The older woman cackled at his discomfort, "You keep calling me Miss and I'll be calling you son before long, sugar. Now, which flavors do y'all want?"

By the time they were finishing their cones, Zoey's heart was feeling significantly lighter, and her sides ached from laughing. It seemed that Dalton's decision to remain in Stone River had eased some of the rift between him and Tanner. Suddenly, anything seemed possible, and she went back to formulating a plan for seducing Tanner. If she could get him into her bed, perhaps she could get him to admit his feelings for her. At which point she would be glad to share her own, and they could talk about what happened next. Until then, she couldn't let herself fall harder for his brothers. It would hurt too much if she was forced to give them all up later.

Tanner accepted the small pint of butter pecan ice cream that Dottie made up for Clint, and tucked it carefully into the cooler surrounded by frozen food so it wouldn't melt. Before they could climb into the truck to leave, a startled gasp slipped from Dalton, and Zoey's heart jumped.

Standing on the sidewalk holding a small bag of charcoal briquettes was Minnie White. Her face was a colorless as her name, and her hands were shaking. Tears filled her eyes, and Zoey's heart broke when she saw Dalton take a step back as if he had been slapped.

"Dalton Keegan?" Minnie whispered. When Dalton nodded and shoved his hands in his pockets, she let out a small laugh. "Oh don't look like that, son. I haven't seen you in so many years...you just look so, grown up!"

His cheeks grew ruddy, and Zoey struggled with what to do. When she would have stepped forward to facilitate the awkward meeting, Tanner wrapped an arm around her waist and pulled her back again. The feeling of his long hot body against her back momentarily fried her brain.

"Hi, Minnie. How are you? How is Walt?" Dalton finally said.

"We're both as good as you would expect. Getting old, but doing okay. I heard you were in Africa?" Minnie said, taking a step closer. Dalton seemed to relax now that he knew she wasn't going to burst into tears.

"Yeah, but I'm back for good now. I'm going to be taking over for Doc Plass." He was holding his breath. Zoey could see the tension in his every muscle.

"That's wonderful news! I'm sure glad to hear it, Dalton. You know, I'd like to have you come over, if you want to. To see Walt, and...to talk." Minnie's words seemed to shock Dalton to the core, and he went pale.

"I don't understand," he said, his eyes jumping to Zoey, who was still held snugly in Tanner's grip. "I thought you two hated me, for not saving —for what happened."

Minnie shook her head, and tears finally started to fall, "Oh no, Dalton! Never once did we hate you! Have you thought that? All of these years? You poor boy! We went through such a hard time when Ben died. There were moments that I wasn't sure we would either one survive it, but if you had gone back for him...well, every day I thank God that you ran for help instead of trying to pull him out. Otherwise we would have been grieving for both of you."

Dalton's eyes grew glassy with unshed tears, and the tension just seemed to drain out of him. "I-I never knew. I thought..."

"Will you come over tonight? Walt and I would really love to spend some time with you if you're not busy, and we're grilling steaks." Minnie glanced toward Zoey and Tanner with a small smile. "Hello, Zoey, Tanner. Do you mind if I steal him away?"

Zoey shook her head, "No, Mrs. White. That's fine, we were just on our way back to the Triple T to put away groceries, but Dalton should go with you. You guys have a few things to talk about."

Dalton gave her a grateful smile, and then nodded. "Yeah, we do."

Zoey accepted a small hand squeeze from Dalton, thankful and slightly disappointed that he didn't offer a more public display of affection. She was, after all, in his brother's arms in full view of the town.

Together, Zoey and Tanner watched him help Minnie to her car and leave with her. It felt as though in a matter of minutes a huge weight had been knocked off their shoulders. Dalton was staying in Stone River. He would have no reservations about it now, and that meant that all three Keegan men would be on the ranch for the rest of the time Zoey was.

Turning to face Tanner, she didn't step away from his grip, she just placed her hand on his chest. "They aren't the only ones that need to talk. I think we do too."

Tanner stared down at her and she watched several emotions dance in his eyes before he took a deep breath and nodded. "Okay, but let's get this stuff home first. If we're going to talk, we're going to do it alone."

Zoey nodded and gave him a quick hug before letting him help her into the truck. The ride home was just as quiet as the ride into town, but the tension had drained away along with the sunshine. As she watched it sinking toward the horizon on the drive, apprehension and excitement warred in her belly. By confronting Tanner, she was either making the biggest move of her life, or the biggest mistake. Only time would tell.

Standing in the kitchen putting groceries away, Zoey had an odd sense of déjà vu as Tanner stood behind her watching, and waiting. Facing him was one of the hardest things she had ever done, but the anxiety on his face eased her own nerves.

Before she could speak, he held his hand out, "Come on, I know where we can go to be alone, and I want to show you something."

Her heart skipped a beat as she placed her hand in his, and a flare of satisfaction lit his eyes. Just that little surrender to him obviously flipped his trigger. What would he do if she fell to her knees and begged him to love her? Tossing her hair over her shoulder, she lifted her chin, "Okay, but I need to let Clint know we're leaving. He'll worry if I don't."

Tanner's head dipped, "Of course. I think he's in the barn, so we can tell him while we saddle the horses."

"Horses?" she asked in confusion.

To see the grin that split his face she would have ridden a horse across the country. "Yes, horses. That's the only way to get to this spot on the ranch."

She followed him out to the barn, their hands still laced together, and her heart racing. Clint was brushing and patiently murmuring to an agitated mama horse when they came in the barn.

"How is she doing?" Tanner asked softly, and Clint glanced up in surprise, taking in their clenched hands with a raised eyebrow.

"Good. I think we'll have a new one by morning." Clint smiled at Zoey, "Hey, angel, did you get everything you needed in town?"

"Yeah, more than we expected."

He stepped out of the stall and brushed a kiss over her lips, "Oh yeah, what else did you find besides groceries?"

"Minnie White." She watched as his face registered the surprise.

"Oh shit. Where is Dalton, is he alright?" Gone was the playful teasing Clint she knew, and in his place stood a concerned brother.

Releasing her grip on Tanner, she stepped closer to Clint, and pressed her hand to his wide chest to ease him, "He's fine. Minnie asked him back to their place to talk. It seems Dalton has been wrong about how they have felt all this time. He'll be back later tonight. Oh, and he took the job from Doc, so I guess he'll be staying permanently."

Clint wrapped his hands around her waist, and swung her in a circle as he laughed, "I knew it! You are an angel! If it weren't for you, none of this would have worked out." His mouth captured hers in a passionate kiss that hinted at deeper emotions. Zoey chose to ignore the reciprocating flutter in her chest as she pulled away from him.

"You're a goof, Hollywood." She was giggling at him, but she stepped back to Tanner's side. The tension in his shoulders seemed to relax a little when her hand slid back into his.

"So that's how it is, huh? Leaving me to run off with my older brother?" Clint said. Tanner inhaled sharply, but Zoey could sense that Clint was just teasing her.

"Yep, but only for a little bit. Tanner wants to show me something on the ranch. You can eat leftovers if you're hungry, or I will fix something when I get back."

Clint's eyes widened and a frown line appeared between them, "Angel, I have been handling myself for a long time, you don't have to worry about taking care of me."

She smiled, "I know, but I like to."

"Well in that case, I'll see you later for dinner." Clint didn't pull her away from the silent Tanner this time, instead he just stepped closer, pinning her between the two of them, and kissing her one more time like his life depended on it. She was stuck between two hard cocks based on the matching ridges behind their zippers, and she moaned with pleasure as her tongue danced with Clint's.

When he finally released her, he met Tanner's eyes with a cocky grin, "Take care of my angel, Skipper. I'm growing pretty attached to her."

Tanner rolled his eyes and snorted before tugging her along behind him to the tack room to collect saddles for their mounts. As they rode out of the barn, Zoey caught a glimpse of Clint watching them from the shadows. He looked nervous and pleased all at once, and her stomach flipped over. This was it. No turning back now. She had to face Tanner head on —once and for all.

After about ten minutes of stewing over what to say, she got fidgety. The sun was almost set, and dusk was upon them. It would be much harder to ride back home in the dark, especially when she wasn't a very experienced rider.

"Are you going to tell me where we're going?" she asked Tanner's broad back with an irritated huff. He looked magnificent in the saddle. His button down shirt hugged his wide shoulders, and stretched over his flexing muscles, while his sexy ass fit the saddle perfectly. She imagined straddling him while he rode, and letting the rocking sway of the horse force his cock deep into her hot pussy. For just a moment her fantasy got the best of her and she faded out. By the time she was aware of her surroundings again, she realized she hadn't even heard whether or not he answered. "I'm sorry, I didn't hear you."

"That's because I didn't answer you, baby. You need to learn patience. Good things come to those who wait." Tanner didn't even turn to acknowledge her while he spoke, he just kept up the same even gate on his mount, like he had nowhere important to be.

"And you need to stop playing mind games. It's getting old."

She might have said more, but they had just topped a small rise and she found herself staring down into a dark hollow of trees. It wasn't unusual to see a spot of trees on the ranch, but smack dab in the center of this cropping was an enormous tree that seemed to be glowing in the dark.

"What is that?" her voice came out a breathless whisper, as awe overwhelmed her earlier ire.

"The glowing tree," Tanner responded, watching her as she took in the spectacle.

"Is the tree actually glowing?" She cocked her head and narrowed her eyes trying to determine the cause of the light. It seemed to be moving all around that one huge oak.

"No, come on, let's get closer."

Tanner nudge her horse ahead of his, and she heard him chuckle when she realized the source of the light. "Fireflies!"

Thousands of the tiny beetle bugs were blinking in the shadows of the oak and its cousin trees. They swarmed over each other in the air in front of the thick trunk, making it look from a distance as though the tree itself was lit up.

"I don't understand. How is this possible? Why are they all here?" she asked, allowing Tanner to help her dismount.

He shrugged, "No one really knows. Pops had some students from the University down here running tests, but they never came up with a good answer. It's just always been like this. Every summer in the evening at dusk you can come out here and find this tree all lit up like it's covered in Christmas lights." He caught one of the glowing bugs as it broke away from its friends, and held it cupped in her hands for her to see. "This used to be the site of an old well, which is why the trees grow so tall right here. There is plenty of water still under ground to sustain them. When they tested the tree, they estimated it to be about a hundred and fifty years old."

Zoey stared up into the glowing ball of creatures in awe. It was a truly magical sight. The sun was barely peeking over the horizon, so very little daylight remained, allowing the bioluminescence of the bugs to be that much brighter. In fact, the greenish yellow glow didn't just light up that one spot. She was able to see into all corners of the small circle of trees. At least fifteen oak trees formed a unique little hollow that allowed the magnificent spectacle to safely occur.

"Why have I never heard about this?" she asked, taking a seat in the grass to watch the fireflies dance.

"It's not like this is easily accessible, and if we started broadcasting that it was here, everyone would want to see it. The Keegan family has always felt like it was our duty to protect it." Tanner sat next to her, leaning his back against one of the smaller trees for support. "I know I hurt you the other night, and I'm sorry. I thought I was doing the right thing by protecting you."

Zoey turned to face him, biting back a sigh as the glow of the fireflies lit his face so that she could see his frown. "I know you weren't trying to hurt me, but it seems like you're always protecting me. Don't you understand that I'm not looking for a knight in shining armor? I want a partner in life, but I want that person to be willing to stand behind me when I need to handle my own business. Sure, I want him to be willing to take up the sword for me if necessary, but that doesn't mean he'll have to."

Tanner shook his head, "You can't have it both ways. I'm a controlling person. I like things in my life to be neat and orderly, and—"

"And you have a strong sense of obligation and responsibility. All of those qualities are things that I love about you," Zoey responded, laying her hand in his, and squeezing him. "What else is stopping you?"

Tanner remained quiet for several moments, and Zoey was afraid he wouldn't answer. When he finally did, his answer surprised her. "I don't know if I can share you."

She stared at him in confusion, "Wait, you didn't want me when I offered myself to you, but now that your brothers want me you don't want to share me?"

"No! Yes! Fuck, I don't know. Look, I think of myself as Dominant in the bedroom."

Zoey's laugh rang out, "Did you think I would turn you away for being bossy in bed?"

"Do you know what Dominant means? It means I have to have

control of certain things, but it mainly means I want my partner's complete trust and I want to protect and coddle her."

She nodded, "Yeah, I know what it means, Tanner. I've read plenty of erotic romances, and I have a few submissive fantasies of my own. What I don't understand is why you think I would turn you away for that."

"I've gone to a local BDSM club with Parker to see if it suited me. It did in some ways, but the biggest thing that it taught me is that I'm not a lifestyle Dom. I like to play, and add elements of BDSM into my sex, but I don't want anyone referring to me as Master, or expecting me to pick out her clothes."

Zoey sighed with relief making Tanner laugh this time. "I'm glad to hear it, because I'm not sure I could call you Master without laughing."

"Fuck, I'm making a mess out of this." He jumped to his feet and began pacing. "Doms don't share."

"Why?" Zoey didn't move from where she sat, but her body was quivering with nerves. Could she possibly make him understand?

"Why? What do you mean why? What kind of Dom would I be if I shared my woman with two other men? With my brothers, no less."

She waited for him to turn and meet her gaze. "Do you think less of Parker for his choice to share Rachel?"

"No, but that's different."

"Uh, pot meet kettle. It is not different. Parker shares Rachel with his brothers because he can see how much she loves them all. He's willing to do what's best for her first and foremost. Have you ever even bothered to talk to him or Rogan, or even Sawyer or Hudson? They will tell you that they make time to be alone with Rachel as well as all together because that's what she needs. Rachel has even gone to The Cage with Parker. They enjoy a little bondage and discipline play occasionally, but the other guys don't as much." Zoey stood and brushed the grass off her butt, "You know, at one time I thought that you were the strongest man I knew. The kind of man who didn't take shit from anyone, and would always be there when he was needed. I need you, Tanner. I need you, Dalton, and Clint, but if I can't have all of you, then I don't want any."

She spun on her heel and walked back to her horse leaving Tanner behind. It took her a couple of tries to get her foot in the stirrup because she was struggling to see clearly through the tears in her eyes, but once she did, she turned her horse and set off for the ranch house. She didn't care that it was dark and she was alone, all that mattered was her desire to escape the pain in her gut. Her make or break moment had broken her heart into millions of pieces. Tanner would never let go of his ideals enough to even try.

A few seconds later the sound of a horse came up hard and fast behind her, startling her and her mount. Turning, she saw the hard line of Tanner's jaw in the moonlight before he reached out and grabbed her reins from her hand.

"I'm not good enough for you, damn it. Don't you get that?" His chest heaved and she stared back in stunned fascination as he glared at her.

"What?"

"I'm a rancher, not some college educated doctor, or anything. I'm just a cowboy who works his fingers to the bone from dawn to dusk. I'm in the saddle just minutes after I swig a pot of coffee, and I fall out of the saddle when the hunger in my belly gets too bad to think straight. Occasionally I want to be able to tie a woman up, and spank her ass, or tease her until we're both mindless. I want her to submit to me, and trust me with every ounce of herself because she knows that all I want is what's best for her. You have to just stay away from me. I know you think that you want me, but you don't deserve this life, Zoey. You deserve so much more."

Refusing to be pushed away, she reached out and pulled the reins back into her grip, "What in the world gave you the idea that I needed a man with a college education to make me happy? And I will gladly let you tie me down and fuck me senseless, spank me, flog me, dominate me. Please! All I have ever wanted is for you to give us a chance. I've wanted you for years, and every time I've gotten close to you, you've pushed me away. Do you know what that does to a girl's self-esteem?"

"I told you I never meant to hurt you. I was trying to protect you. I am happy for you and my brothers, but I can't get in the middle of it. Those two are what you need."

"You're right, I do want Dalton," Zoey said softly, and her heart clenched when Tanner's strong shoulders drooped in defeat.

"But I want you too, and for the record, I want Clint as well. Yes, I know that's stingy, and ridiculous, and maybe it all started out of pure jealousy over my best friend having four hot men—" A low growl rumbled out of his chest. "Oh shut up, they are hot, but not as hot as you three. Maybe I started out wanting to try a ménage, and ended up finding out that I need it too. I want all three of you. For the long haul, however we can make it work. I don't care if you're in the saddle six days a week, as long as at night you're in my bed, and on Sundays you make time for me. Don't you get it you jackass? I love you."

Tanner's jaw dropped open, and he and his horse came to a dead stop. Zoey slowed her own horse, and turned to face him. Moving closer so she could see the expression on his face in the faint light, she waited for the hammer to drop. She had admitted her feelings for him, now he would go running.

"Tanner?"

He lifted his gaze to meet hers, and she had to take a deep breath at the heat in his eyes. "Sundays, huh?"

"Sundays. All day long."

They stared each other down for a few more moments before she spoke again. "You were my rock, Tanner, when everything else in my world fell apart I was able to come to you for unconditional help. I don't care what you do for a living, or where you've been or will go in your life, but I won't accept you saying you aren't good enough for me. Period. You have been my protector for too long, now it's up to you to make the choice to be my lover too."

He leaned over, and took her chin between his thumb and forefinger, forcing her to lean to the side in her saddle to meet him in a kiss. Their lips smashed together, teeth clashing, tongues battling, and Zoey's pussy wept for joy.

When they finally pulled apart they were both panting for air and Tanner was grinning. "We need to get home, so I can show you just how much that means to me, baby."

Turning her horse, she laughed, "Then what are we waiting for, cowboy? Let's go!"

As much as Zoey wanted to gallop across the grass to the ranch house, she knew it wasn't safe in the dark. Instead, she followed his lead slowly but carefully back home. Once there, he took both horses from her and pressed a quick kiss to her mouth. "My room, fifteen minutes."

## CHAPTER TEN

Tanner unsaddled and stalled the horses faster than he ever had before. His cock was throbbing in his jeans, and his blood felt electrified as it pumped through his brain. Zoey was going to be his for tonight. He was finally going to get the chance to touch and taste every sexy inch of her lush body, and then sink into her tight pussy.

Stifling a groan at the wicked images racing through his brain, he adjusted his wood behind his zipper and headed for his bedroom. The door was closed, and when he pushed it open he was pleased to see that she followed his instructions. Her apprehension was clear in the way she sat stiffly on the edge of the bed, but there was hope and desire in her gorgeous blue eyes, and she held the red rose he had given her in her hands. He couldn't get over how sexy it was to see her in his bedroom. The anticipation of having her was quite possibly the hottest thing he had ever experienced.

He moved to her side quickly, and stood over her, invading her space to see how she handled it. Her head tilted back, and he saw her throat convulse around a nervous swallow. Gently tugging the rose from her hands, he ran his fingertips over the soft petals. "Why did you bring this in here, Zoey?"

"I-I'm not exactly sure." Her eyes darted away from him when he gave her a hard look of disbelief.

"I guess I wanted to be sure that you remembered to be romantic. I've fantasized about Dominance and submission, but I've never experienced it. I'm a little scared now."

Tanner ran the crimson flower over her soft cheek, and then her lips, smiling slightly when she inhaled as it passed under her nose. "You have nothing to be scared of, baby. We'll only go as far and as fast as you are up to. Trust me."

She gave him a tentative nod, and then tipped her chin back to look up at him again. "Um, so what now?"

If it weren't for the butterflies dancing in his own stomach, he might have laughed. She was such an interesting blend of vixen and virgin that it kept him on his toes. The woman who had blatantly teased and challenged him hadn't waited to triumph; she had disappeared behind a veil of self-conscious nerves.

"Now, I teach you patience. You say you've fantasized about submitting to me, and now you will experience it. In the morning we'll talk and you can decide whether or not you want to continue, or bail." He tugged the elastic from her hair, letting her ponytail free, tangling his fingers in the heavy locks, and then he tugged on it. Her gasp made his dick pulse.

Her eyes drifted shut, but before they did he saw the sparkle nearly snuffed out. "So this is one night..."

"No." The one word answer came out harsher than he intended, but it did have her snapping her eyes open again. "No, I want this to be more than that. I don't want you to think that you're an easy screw for me, baby. You are so much more than that. I just don't think you know what you're getting yourself into yet."

Those brilliant blue eyes of hers seemed to penetrate the layers of self-loathing, and self-denial, reaching deep into his heart and laying it wide open. "Give it your best shot, cowboy. I'm not leaving until you push me out."

A growly groan broke free from his voice box, and he pushed her onto her back on his bed, and set the flower down nearby. Taking his time, he ran his hands over her clothed form, pressing kisses to her mouth, nose, chin, jaw, and every inch of skin he exposed as he peeled her shirt over her head. He bit his own tongue when he flipped open the front clasp of her bra and bared her creamy breasts to his view. Her nipples were about the size of dimes, but the areolas were large and a delicious dusky rose color.

As he reverently skimmed his lips over her ribcage, she arched up into him and tried to grab his head. He jerked backwards, and pushed her hands down into the mattress underneath her. "No, baby. Lesson number one, I'm in charge. You take what I give you."

Zoey nodded, her pupils expanding as her desire increased. She was a feast for sore eyes with her lush curves and milky white skin, spread out on his dark navy blue comforter. An innocence to her eager responses and the pink blush of need that covered her skin struck a chord in his chest.

Standing tall between her spread knees, he pulled his shirt off over his head, pleased when she licked her lips at the sight of his naked torso. Her eyes skirted over the curly hair between his nipples, and then followed the dark line down to the button of his jeans. Before she could stop him, he reached out and tugged her pants down over her hips without even releasing the closure. She let out a strangled moan that matched his own when he caught sight of her lack of panties.

"Fuck me, baby. You were going commando this whole time? If I had known that I would have pulled your jeans down back at the tree and spanked your bare ass for all of the fireflies to see, just before I fucked you silly."

Her thighs spread and a cloud of arousal perfumed the air around them. His mouth watered to get a taste of her, but he resisted. The edge was too close to take a chance. Instead, he finished undressing her, and then took a seat on the bed patting his thigh. When Zoey hesitated, he gave her a hard look. "I'll give you one more chance, baby. Get your ass in the air, and prepare for your punishment."

"Punishment? What am I being punished for?" She sounded so indignant, and when she stood up quickly her pert breasts bounced, distracting him for a moment.

"For all of your teasing and flirting. If you've read any good BDSM story then you know that's topping from the bottom and I won't tolerate it." He kept his voice even so as not to alert her to the effect she had on his cock, but when she suddenly looked nervous again, he softened, "And because I want to see your sexy ass turn pink under my hand. I want to feel you squirm in my lap, and I want to know how far I can push you before you beg me to make love to you."

Flames flared up in her eyes, and her lips parted on an exhale. It was just the reaction he hoped for as she moved to stretch over his lap. Helping her adjust into place, she wriggled into a comfortable spot that put the perfect curve of her ass right where he wanted it. He could feel the tension in her muscles as she explored something new, and the vulnerability of her position set in.

The skin of her bare back was softer than satin as he delicately danced one hand over her from the base of her neck to the split of her ass, all while keeping the other hand firmly planted on the back of her upper thigh. Holding her, securing her, but not giving her what she wanted, he relished in the sensation of having her naked in his hands.

When she finally began to relax under his touch, he gave her a light tap on the softest part of her rump to test the waters. Her gasp, and sigh, was exactly what he was hoping for, and he brought his hand down again, on the opposite cheek this time.

Rubbing to ease the burn of impact, he pushed his fingers up between the lips of her pussy to find her dripping wet. "My baby likes a little sting, huh?"

She didn't respond verbally, but her head dropped in submission. It told him that she was absolutely invested in the moment. As he gave her a few more swats, and she hissed out a sharp breath, he wondered if he should have discussed limits and safewords with her first. It was a hard fast rule at The Cage, the BDSM club he had visited with Parker, but in this case he didn't think he would ever be able to push Zoey so far out of her comfort zone that she would need it. And he knew tonight he certainly wouldn't last that long. Tonight he was more focused on giving her everything she asked for, without ever asking.

Turning her in his arms, he cradled her against his chest like a child.

Her tender ass rubbing against the rough material of his jeans and making her flinch a little.

"Please, Tanner!"

Her begging made his balls ache, and he kissed her forehead. "Not yet, baby. That was just a little appetizer to test the waters. We haven't even started on the main course."

She went where he guided her, lying back in the middle of the bed and allowing him to put her arms above her head. He pressed them to the pillows and gave her a quick wink. "Leave these here."

Picking up the rose again, he ran the soft petals over her equally soft skin making her shiver. He kissed his way down her curvy legs to her toes and gently ran the flower over the soles of her bare feet, kissing the arch. When she giggled he narrowed his eyes at her. "What?"

"That tickles, stop." The blush on her cheeks told him there was more.

"Why don't you like me playing with your sexy feet, baby?" he asked, gripping her foot firmly in one hand and rubbing his thumb hard down the arch to make her groan.

"They aren't sexy, they are enormous," she hissed out, arching her back up off the bed as he slid the stem of the flower between her toes, careful not to prick her with a thorn.

Tanner shook his head, "There is nothing too big about you, baby. You are sexy as hell from the top of your head to the tips of your toes, and I happen to find your feet very erotic."

Lifting himself to a better angle, he settled her feet into his lap, and proceeded to massage them, alternating between pressing them against his erection and teasing her with a thrusting motion of the stem between her toes. She began to writhe uncontrollably after a few minutes, begging him to ease the burning need inside of her.

Dropping the flower to the floor, he used his palms to spread her thighs, opening her to his mouth. Without any more build up, he descended on her tender flesh and carried her to greater heights. Her hips rocked and her thighs clenched tight around his ears when she exploded against his face. The sound of his name from her lips did his precious control in.

As much as he wanted to continue to play with her, his cock was going to embarrass him if he didn't fuck her. He grabbed a condom from his bedside table and quickly sheathed his aching erection while she was still mellow from her orgasm.

The fat head of his cock spread her swollen pussy lips creating an erotic picture that was branded into his memories. He knew that any future jacking off would be to this one moment in time when her body lay submissively splayed for his pleasure, and her pussy dripped with her desire.

Arching his larger frame over her, he laced his hands with hers and met her heavy lidded gaze before forcing his thickness into her tight channel. Her gasp was followed by a full body undulation that sent a zap of electricity up his spine and back down to his balls. By the time he had worked his dick fully into her tight pussy, he was panting and sweat was dripping down his back.

"You feel like heaven, baby," he whispered to her, allowing his emotions to show in his eyes as much as possible. In this moment, it wasn't about Dominance or submission. It was just about making love to the woman that his heart and soul craved. It was about bringing them both to the glorious heights they could only achieve together, and strengthening the bond between their spirits. Never before had he wanted so badly to say the "L" word to anyone, and it was on the tip of his tongue as he thrust into her body, slaking his need and hers.

His knees slid under her hips, propping her up so his cock rubbed against the small spot deep inside of her that he knew would drive her crazy and using their connected hands as his anchor, he fucked her with every bit of unsaid emotion in his heart.

Somehow she understood. Her blue eyes widened, and her puffy lips parted on a moan, just before those same lips curved up in a wicked smile, and she tightened on his dick.

This time when she screamed his name, he echoed her cries with his own, feeling something inside of him release, and his heart finally ease. He was home.

## CHAPTER ELEVEN

Zoey's eyes closed tightly when she climaxed, and her ears filled with the sound of Tanner calling out her name as he found his own release. It was the most beautiful sound in the world, and it took her breath away.

It took a few seconds for the sharp sound of clapping to register in her head, but when it did, she jerked in surprise to find Clint and Dalton watching from the bedroom doorway with mile wide smiles on their faces.

"That was epic, Skipper," Clint said as he continued his applause.

Tanner acted like a scalded cat as he jumped away from her, his condom nearly pulling off his now drooping cock in the process. He recovered it and quickly dropped the spent rubber in the trashcan, using his discarded shirt to clean himself up. When he finished he stepped into his bathroom and grabbed a hand towel. She jumped when he pushed her thighs apart and cleaned her up.

"Thank you," she murmured, staring up into his amber gaze feeling more than a little sad at his reluctance to include his brothers in their moment.

She could see the war of emotions in his eyes, and when he finally sighed and dropped down to sit next to her, she was relieved. "What the hell are you two doing? This wasn't a show for your voyeuristic pleasure, you know?"

"Well it might not have started out that way, but I'm damn sure glad I made it back home in time to catch the finale," Dalton said. He came directly to her, unhindered by his brother's nude form next to him as he pressed a kiss to her lips. "Hey, pretty lady, you look delicious."

It was impossible not to return his grin, "I feel pretty damn delicious right now."

Clint appeared on her other side, and instead of kissing her mouth, he leaned over her torso and sucked her nipple between his lips hard, and then let it go with a loud pop. "Mmm, you taste pretty yummy too." Her giggle made him smile before he brought his lips to hers. His gentle butterfly kiss over her lips made her sigh with pleasure. "Guess this means dinner will be delayed, huh?"

She snorted, "Ya think? I can't even feel my legs yet." Tanner gave her a small smirk of satisfaction but didn't say anything. Ignoring the sting of hurt in her heart, she turned to Dalton. "So how did it go with the White's?"

"You really want to talk about *that* now?" he asked with a groan. When she gave him a hard look, he sighed and then smiled. "It went great. Better than I could have dreamed. I had a lot of things wrong for so many years, and they thought that I was avoiding them because it hurt too much to see them. Now it's all in the open, and they seem really glad to have me back in town. Thank you, Zoey."

"Hey, I didn't do anything!" she protested, trying to sit up, but Clint's weight held her in place.

"You encouraged me to keep an open mind, and in this case, that's all I needed." He kissed her again, and then gestured to Tanner, "So what does this mean for all of us?"

Zoey looked to Tanner who sat silently next to her staring at his hands. His shoulders were taut with tension, but his head was bowed. "Tanner?"

"I told you I wasn't sure if I could share…"

She flinched, as if he had physically lashed out at her. "But, I thought…what the fuck was all of this then?"

Shock filled his eyes at her anger, "No, baby, that's not what I'm saying. Let me finish! What I wanted to say is that even though I'm not sure how we'll make it all work, I want to try. To be honest, I don't think I can give you up after having a taste of you."

Warmth filled her belly soothing the sting of his earlier silence, and she let him take her hand between his, pressing a kiss to her palm. Clint pinched her nipple making her yelp, and laugh, "Yep, once you've had a hit of our angel, you can't resist coming back for more. That's what brought me to your bedroom door. Well, that and the sexy fuck noises the two of you were making. I almost blew my load when you two did."

Tanner snorted and rolled his eyes, while Zoey and Dalton both laughed. Her eyes bounced from man to man as she searched for answers to the hundreds of questions running through her brain. If they were serious, then she might just lose her mind trying to sort out all of the hurdles they faced.

Settling on the issue that currently fogged her brain, she moved her hands up to cup her own breasts. "I have one big question..." Pausing for effect, she arched her back and pinched her own nipples, "Which one of you is going to give me my next orgasm?"

They were all laughing as Dalton and Clint stripped their clothes and joined her and Tanner on the king size bed. This time, Tanner slid up behind her, supporting her against his chest as he recovered from their monumental orgasm of a few moments ago. She nearly purred when his hands came around to replace hers on her breasts, offering them to Dalton and Clint as though a meal on a platter. "Have another taste, guys. I think Zoey wants to test her limits tonight, and we're just the men to help her with that."

Clint didn't waste much time on her breasts before moving down her body with his hot mouth. He ran his tongue over the rise of her rib cage making her giggle, and then it dipped into the hollow of her belly button and skirted the curve of her hip. By the time he reached the top of her soaked pussy, she was whimpering.

One hand found the back of his head when his fingers spread her labia and he blew air over her swollen clit. "Fuck, Clint!"

Tanner's hands released her tits to grab her wrists, tugging them to her side and holding her in place while his brothers feasted on her body. "No you don't, baby, if you want all of us, then you get us as we are." His words sent tingles washing over her, and she moaned, letting her legs fall open wider to give Clint more access.

Hot skin pressed along her cheek as she turned her face in an attempt to bite Tanner's nipple. His hiss of irritation blew across her face, and he let out a low growl. "You're playing with fire, Zoey. I've already spanked you once, don't push me."

He didn't seem to understand that that was exactly what she wanted to do. She wanted to push him outside of his comfort zone, and shake him up. Everything was new to her, and it kept her hanging by an uncomfortable thread of anxiety as she tried to absorb each new experience, but she wanted them to understand and feel that too. "I want you. All of you."

Dalton's head shot up from where he had been masterfully plying her breasts, and he grabbed her chin in his hand to look her in the eye. "Do you know what you're asking for, kitten?"

There was an almost imperceptible layer of doubt in his eyes, and she saw it slip away when she nodded, "Yes, if nothing else ever happens between us again, I want to experience it all tonight. I want one of you in my pussy, and one in my ass while I suck the third."

All three men stopped what they were doing and awkwardly exchanged silent communication before Clint frowned at her, "Have you ever had anal sex, angel?"

Her gaze darted away from his, and suddenly Dalton was in her face while Tanner held her still, "Answer him, kitten. This is important."

"Not with someone," she whispered, and she caught the blazing look of shock and desire that fired his blue eyes.

Tanner shifted behind her, his hard cock pressing into her ribs from the back. "Are you saying you've masturbated with anal play?"

The blush was fast, and it heated her face as her core reached boiling point and she gave him a short nod. All three men groaned deeply and seemed to retreat to regroup.

Tanner lifted her and turned her around in one quick motion so she was forced to straddle his thick thighs and rest her palms on his muscular chest to support herself. "Baby, that is the sexiest thing I've ever heard, and someday I fully intend on watching you pleasure yourself that way, but for tonight, you get to experience it all."

She accepted his kiss as he stole away every single reservation that still lingered in her brain and relaxed against him. When their lips parted, Dalton grabbed her by the hair and tugged her head back to kiss her himself. Inches apart, neither man wavered as they accepted each other's right to be there touching her so intimately.

Clint, of course, had no reservations, and she jumped when his tongue ran down the split of her ass. Tanner's hands pressed her hips back down to his lap, so she was spread wide for the younger Keegan brother's attentions. From behind, Clint's fingers sunk into her dripping channel, pulling her own cream from her body and using it to ease the tight muscles of her ass.

It was nearly impossible to focus on what he was doing as Tanner manipulated her breasts, pinching and pulling them hard enough to make her gasp at the sharp pleasure and intense heat. Dalton's mouth ravished hers, swallowing her noises and her need as he caressed and fucked her mouth with his own.

She heard Tanner tell Clint there was lube in the nightstand drawer, and then she heard the click of a cap just before icy cold moisture joined his fingers on her asshole. There was no escaping the insistent pressure of his fingers as they pushed past the ring of muscles into her bowel.

"Holy shit, she's tight. She's going to strangle my cock when I get it in there. Easy, angel, I'm just going to stretch you a little." Clint's voice was tight with need, and Zoey forced her muscles to relax around him allowing him to penetrate her backside further. "That's it, let me in."

Their triple shot of concern and encouragement sent her desire even higher, and she felt herself rocking back on Clint's fingers for more. As he slid a second and then a third finger into her body, she whimpered and bit Dalton's lip so she could take a breath.

When he pulled back just a few inches, she gave him her best sexy look and resorted to begging, "Please, I need more."

Another silent exchange happened between the brothers, but lust fogged her brain enough that she was having difficulty keeping up with their movements. Quickly she found herself being manipulated until she blanketed Tanner's whole body. Clint's fingers were still pulsing in and out of her ass, but now Tanner was on his back so his cock pressed against her weeping pussy. Dalton knelt on the bed next to them and brought her hand up to fist his erection. She used her thumb to spread the moisture pooled on the head, and he moaned.

Tanner groaned when she tried to shift so she could line up his dick with her aching channel. "Fuck, Clint, you better get your dick inside of her quick, or she's going to be too full of me to take you."

She felt Clint moving behind her so he was between Tanner's spread legs. His hand flattened on her back, forcing her forward until her tits were scraping over his older brother's bare chest, sending fire through her body again.

Clint's fingers slid free of her ass, and then his thick cockhead pressed against her anus. Forcing his way past the impossibly tight ring of muscles, he groaned along with her. It was nothing like being full of a plastic dildo. The burning feeling was intense and it ran from her asshole to her fingertips and back. Her breathing came out in gasps as she tried to force herself to relax and let him inside of her.

Tanner's hands came up to hold her head still, his large palms bracketing her flushed cheeks, "Easy, baby, breathe. Relax and bear down, let Clint in. You want this, you want us to fill you up, so relax and enjoy it."

His focus on calming her emotions, allowed her to regain her control, and she did what he instructed. Her body easing to allow Clint to sink deeper into her backside. "Christ, you are fucking incredible, Zoey."

"Back-atcha, Hollywood," she moaned as his pubic hair tickled her ass cheeks, and then he eased his long, hard cock out of her, before sinking in again. Slowly she relaxed around him, then with another quick squirt of lube he was sliding in and out of her more easily, and pushing her to the edge of climax.

"No you don't, baby," Tanner snarled. Zoey popped her eyes open to find his liquid gold gaze blazing with heat. "I want in that pussy before you come."

This time when she shifted to line up her cunt with his cock, he let her. Her opening stretched around his thick shaft but with Clint inside of her ass, it was almost impossible to breathe through his entry. Focusing on

Tanner's full lips, which were set in a determined grimace, she pushed herself to relax.

A groan from her left had her glancing at Dalton. Her fist was still wrapped around his erection, but she wasn't moving it. Instead, she was just locked on him like a vise as she concentrated on his brothers. He caught her looking and winked, "Don't worry about me, kitten, I'm enjoying the show. I'll catch up in a couple of minutes."

The distraction was enough to allow Tanner to push his way into her body. Completely full of two of her three men, she could hear herself whimpering as she let sensation wash over her. They quickly worked out a rhythm between them, taking turns easing in and out of her body, giving her an unending stream of fulfillment. Her own blood seemed to be burning her up from the inside out as she fought to stay conscious through all of their ministrations.

When Dalton brought his cock to her lips and rubbed his sticky cock head against her, she parted them instinctively. His unique taste hit her tongue and she swallowed around him. He kept his thrusts shallow, so as not to distract her more from all of the other events happening, but he wrapped his hand in her hair to hold her head steady. It was the ultimate moment of bliss and submission for her. Her men took over and she just relaxed into their possession. Never again would she experience this for the first time. It might be good again in the future, but it would never compete with the feeling of acceptance that filled her as her climax broke free and swamped her like a tidal wave.

Later she would have to admit that she didn't remember Dalton pulling free of her mouth and coming in his fist, or Tanner and Clint coming deep inside her body. Delicious pleasure swamped her, blinding her to everything but the acceptance of pure sexual hedonism, and she fainted.

---

Later, she awoke tangled in a mass of sweaty sheets and masculine limbs with Clint sound asleep underneath her cheek. She allowed herself the opportunity to admire him while he slept. From his chiseled jaw and dimpled chin down the long sweep of his throat where his pulse beat steadily, and even further still to the wide chest that dipped and curved with only ridges of muscles breaking the solid plane. His build was significantly bulkier than either Tanner or Dalton, and for the hundredth time since he appeared back on the Triple T she wondered how Hollywood had missed out on this magnificent man.

When he smiled, everyone nearby smiled with him. It was almost as if his duty to the world was to create joy, so it only made sense that he might do that on screen or on stage. Instead, the bright lights and craving for fame had broken him and knocked his knees out from underneath him.

She had observed him as he stepped back into the cowboy boots that he left behind and took up the reins of the cowboy lifestyle again. He was like a drop of sunshine on the withered plants, and already she had noticed a more relaxed air around the other ranch hands. He had a natural ability for reading both humans and animals, and his determination to shine a positive light on everything around him was one of the biggest things that she admired about him.

In the back of her mind she thought about what it would be like to have Clint as the father of her children and a life partner. There would never be a dull moment, and her children would never be faced with feeling unloved or unwanted. Wasn't that exactly what she had always dreamed of? As the image of miniature Keegan offspring filled her brain, her heart stuttered in her chest.

Tanner hadn't used a condom when they had sex the second time. That was exactly what she didn't want for herself and her future offspring. If these three men committed to her, she wanted it to be because they couldn't live without her, not because of some misplaced sense of obligation to her and an unplanned pregnancy.

Clint seemed to sense her sudden tension in his sleep, his arm tightened around her midsection, and he shifted to press his face into her hair, inhaling deeply.

"You okay, angel?" he murmured sleepily into her ear.

She nodded, but the emotional dam holding back all of her fears and worries was cracking. All it took was him rising up on one elbow and staring down into her eyes with a deep concern for her she wasn't used to, and the dam broke. Tears filled her eyes and her chest sagged with a heavy sob.

"Oh shit, Zoey! What's wrong, angel? Did we hurt you? Are you okay?" His immediate panic struck a chord in her chest and she sobbed harder.

Through her hiccupping cries she managed to mumble, "I'm fine, just emotional. This has been a rough week for me."

The muscles in his body seemed to relax by a few degrees, and he tugged her over until she was draped over him like a small child. Her head tucked under his chin, and her legs slid between his spread thighs, so she was surrounded by the comfort he could give. "I know it has, angel. I'm sorry for that. Me and the guys just had to work through all of the kinks before we could address how much we all three wanted you."

"It's not just you guys. I've been trying to figure out what to do about my job, and where I'm going to live, and falling for three cowboys certainly changes any decisions I might make about both of those things."

He held her in his arms, his strong heartbeat slowly calming her violent emotional outburst. When she was tearless and barely hiccupping, he spoke again. "Don't freak me out like that, doll. I'm not good with crying, it kinda messes with my head."

She giggled against his collarbone and pressed a kiss to the pulse throbbing in his neck. "I'm sorry. I'm not sure why I flipped like that. Everything just hit me all at once. I never imagined I would be considering sharing my body with three brothers."

"Hopefully we made it good enough for you that you want to come back for more later." His smug look of masculine satisfaction nearly had her denying it just to rile him, but instead she chose to stroke his ego with honesty.

"You couldn't keep me away." Relaxing into his gentle touch, she followed his hands as they stroked up her back to the nape of her neck, and back down to the base of her ass in a comforting sort of petting. "Clint, are you happy here? Back at the Triple T? Do you miss California?"

For a moment she didn't think he would answer her, and when he took an enormous breath and let it all out in a whoosh, she started to shift away. His hands clamped down over her round ass cheeks and he growled a little. The sound was so unlike Clint that she felt her mouth drop open in surprise.

"I don't miss California, because everything I want and need is in Texas." Her sensitive female pride sufficiently flattered, she dropped her head back to his chest to listen. "Out there, I was surrounded by beautiful women, and powerful people, but I was also surrounded by con artists, and people so desperate to hold their dreams in their hands that they would do anything to get it. And I do mean anything. I'm not that person. I'm pretty easy going. I figure if life hands you lemons, consider it an offer to partake in body shots and find some Tequila."

Laughter shook her, "That's limes. You do body shots with limes."

"Hey, you do shots your way, and I'll do them mine. The point is, that I was naïve and ridiculously ignorant of how to work the business. I don't play politics very well, and coming back to the Triple T was probably the only thing that saved my life. Believe it or not, I have spent the last four months or so on anti-depressants. The doctor said that my depression was a chemical imbalance, and once the medicine got into my system it went a long way toward me regaining my optimistic attitude."

This time she sat up completely to stare down at him in wonder, "I can't believe you of all people were depressed! You were chasing your dreams, and making a good living, how could you be depressed?"

"Depression isn't always about bad shit happening to ya. Sometimes it's just a matter of not being able to cope with every day things. Anyway, I knew from the moment I saw your perky round ass be-bopping around the kitchen that first day that I had to have you, no matter what." He pulled her down for a quick kiss, and when she was distracted, he rolled her, switching their positions. Even though he settled between her thighs, the move wasn't sexual, somehow he used it to make her feel cherished. For the first time she began to suspect there were more layers to Clint just as she had found out with Dalton and Tanner.

"I'm glad you aren't easily put off your mission." She said with a laugh, "I can't imagine being any luckier than I am right now in this moment."

"We're the lucky ones, angel. Tanner filled us in on how he treated you years ago when you approached him. I'm surprised you even gave any of us the time of day after being shit on like that." Clint's irritation on her behalf made her belly tingle, and she lifted her head to kiss him.

"Thank you, but I believe everyone deserves a second chance, and even sometimes a third. Now, you better let me up because I have to pee like a racehorse and you're on my bladder." His laughter echoed through the room as he rolled away allowing her to dart into the bathroom.

She would never get tired of hearing that sound, or feeling his eyes on her as she moved. If this was what her future looked like, then she welcomed it with open arms.

By the time she came out of the bathroom, Clint had pulled on some sweats, and he held out a robe to her. "Slip this on and we'll go find the guys. They are supposed to be making something for us to eat, but considering the lack of culinary talent between the two of them, we're probably going to end up with peanut butter and jelly."

"I'm more of a peanut butter and honey girl," she responded, allowing him to take her hand and lead her into the living room.

Tanner was slicing a brick of cheese, while Dalton was filling a tray with some summer sausage and crackers. They both looked up with smiles on their faces as she entered the room.

"Hey, baby, Clint was supposed to let you sleep," Tanner said, nuzzling her temple when she stepped to his side and hugged him briefly.

"He did. I was the one who woke him up." She moved to Dalton and hugged him.

"More like she had a nervous breakdown on me," Clint said with a snort.

Immediately Tanner and Dalton turned their complete attention on her. "What's wrong, kitten?"

She rolled her eyes, "Nothing, it's no big deal. I just had a little cry."

"She's worried about her job, and whether or not she's going to move out of here." She sent Clint a nasty look as he spilled her secrets.

"Tattletale," she hissed at him, but he just winked in response.

"Well, I can ease part of those fears, you're not moving anywhere, baby. Not unless you want to," Tanner said, putting down his knife to give her a kiss.

"I second that, and as far as your job goes, I think you should tell Helen to kiss your ass when you see her tomorrow," Dalton said.

"I can't do that, I need a job," Zoey argued, accepting a bottle of water from Clint as the other two finished their tasks and they all moved to the living room.

"There are other jobs out there," Clint said with a shrug.

"But this is my dream. I want to help kids."

Clint's eyes met hers and he gave her a wistful smile, "Someone once told me that trying for your dream and failing is better than never trying at all. Maybe it's time your dream changed. You can help kids some other way. You shouldn't have to tolerate that woman's nastiness."

Zoey's eyes filled with tears, and she moved to Clint, settling in his lap and kissing him deeply. For a moment they were lost in the intense emotions passing between them, and when they broke apart, she pressed her forehead to his, whispering, "Thank you."

"You're welcome, but it's partially out of my own selfishness. I would much rather the woman I love be happy when she comes home from work."

"I love you too, Clint," she answered.

"Zoey, I know I should have pulled my head out of my ass much sooner, but I do love you. I think I've been in love with you since before that horrible night at Robin's," Tanner said.

"You sure have a funny way of showing it, cowboy," she smarted off, but she grinned at him to ease the sting of her attitude. "I love you too, Tanner."

"And me? What about me, pretty lady?" Dalton said, giving her wide puppy dog eyes.

"Hmm...I'm still on the fence about you..."

They all laughed, and Dalton kissed her hard on the mouth. "I love you too, kitten. More than I ever imagined possible."

"Enough to play doctor later maybe?" she asked with a wiggle of her eyebrows. He tickled her until she cried mercy, "I love you too, Professor."

They all settled in to eat their makeshift dinner before making love into the wee hours of the morning. Zoey told herself that she was going to take it all one day at a time, and accept whatever fate tossed on her plate, but in truth, she knew that she was so deeply in love with all three Keegan brothers that she couldn't walk away from them if she tried.

Perhaps Clint was right, and it was time for a new dream and a new beginning.

## CHAPTER TWELVE

THE QUARTET MANAGED to enjoy one week of blissful happiness, going about their lives and virtually playing house before the bottom dropped out. At six a.m. Monday morning, one week into her life with the Keegan brothers, Zoey's phone rang while she was pouring pancake batter on the hot griddle. The sharp chirping sound startled her and she bumped her wrist against the pan, sending a flare of pain all the way up her elbow.

"Shit-fucker!" she gasped as she dropped the bowl and ladle she had been using on the counter, and rushed to the sink to run cold water over her burn.

A moment later, she heard Tanner's voice rumbling from the bedroom where her phone was still plugged in on the nightstand. She had left Dalton sleeping in the bed, while Tanner was showering. It was Clint's night to sleep on his own, because there was barely enough room in Tanner's king size bed for three of them. Tanner claimed that because it was his bed, he didn't have to give up his spot against her backside, so Dalton and Clint rotated who got dibs on snuggling her front. It felt right to have Tanner at her back while she slept. And for the first time in years she slept soundly, relaxed in the comfort of his and his brother's protective embrace.

They were going to order a new bed soon, but Tanner wanted to knock out a wall between her old bedroom and the master first to enlarge it. Zoey had halted that plan for the moment, but only because she felt they needed a little more time before they started major remodeling plans. It concerned her that they hadn't told their parents about their relationship yet, and for that matter, most of Stone River still didn't know. As much as she loved them, she felt like they needed to move slowly as they learned about how a polyamorous relationship should work.

Patting her injury dry, she shut off the stove and scraped the now scorched pancake off the griddle into the trashcan. Before she resumed her routine of cooking breakfast for her men she figured she better find out who in the world was calling her before dawn had even cleared the treetops.

The moment she saw Tanner's face, she knew something wasn't right. He stood next to the bed, with a towel slung around his lean hips, and the phone to his ear. A dark grimace shadowed his visage, and she pressed a fist to her stomach as she moved closer.

"Tanner? Who is it?"

He turned to face her, with worry and fear in his eyes. Her knees trembled beneath her, and she nearly stopped breathing. Dalton was just coming awake at the noise surrounding him, but his body went on instant alert when he caught on to their tension.

"Zoey, kitten, sit down before you fall. Tanner, what the hell is going on? Who is that?" Dalton's hands pulled her down until she sat on the edge of the bed. A steady shivering feeling was building in her muscles, and he began running his hands up and down her arms as though to warm her.

Tanner asked the caller to hold on for a moment, and he held the phone against his ripped abs. For just a moment Zoey let herself focus in on a bead of water as is raced its way down his body, between his pecks, and over the glorious ridges of muscles until it soaked up into the terry cloth material that hugged his Adonis belt. What she wouldn't give to be that drop of water right now.

"Baby, listen to me. This is the police department in Wichita, Kansas. They are calling because your mom was taken to the hospital yesterday by ambulance." She heard herself gasp, but she honestly didn't feel anything. It was as if a cold, dark void settled in the middle of her chest, and stole her heart and her voice away. "Zoey, she overdosed. She's in critical condition and they just now managed to track you down as her next of kin."

A loud roaring sound filled her ears, and suddenly she felt like she was racing through a never ending tunnel. Tanner wasn't talking to her anymore. No one was. All she could focus on was the white terry cloth material against his caramel colored skin. Was Dalton still holding her? Yes, she could feel the pressure of his hands, but not the warmth. There was no warmth left in the room. Only ice cold numbness.

"Zoey, did you hear me?" Tanner snapped at her, and she felt the odd sense of disassociation break free. Lifting her head, she nodded at him.

"I need to go to Wichita." The words were soft, but steady, and she silently patted herself on the back for her lack of emotion. After what Eve did to her, she really didn't deserve any more than that from her daughter.

Dalton spoke next to her ear, "No, pretty lady, *we* need to go to Wichita."

Tanner was speaking into the phone again, confirming with the police department that he would bring his wife to Wichita as quickly as possible. The only thing Zoey heard was the word wife. She gave him an odd look as he hung up the phone and dropped the towel to tug on a pair of boxer briefs. To her surprise he took a seat on the bed on the opposite side of her from Dalton and wrapped his arms around her.

"It's gonna be okay, baby. I know it's a shock, but we'll get on the first plane out of here. We're going to get you there to see her." He spoke to her like a child, while he rubbed her back and shoulder. His fidgety movements in direct contrast to the calm strength in his voice.

"You told them I was your wife." It was a statement, not a question or accusation, but Tanner flinched when she said it.

"Yeah sorry, when it was a man on the phone asking for you at six in the morning I got a little jealous. I might have said that you were my wife and anything concerning you concerned me too. It's nearly true. Or at least it will be true in the near future. I hope you're not too pissed at me for it."

She shook her head, and then turned to Dalton, "Will you get Clint?"

He nodded and bounded out of the bed and down the hallway without even pausing to put on clothes. The image of his naked ass running out of the room might have been humorous in any other situation, but right now it only served to ratchet up the tension in her body.

Tanner gripped her chin in his hand and kissed her hard on the mouth. When he pulled back he searched her eyes for something before speaking again, "Baby, talk to me. What's going on in that pretty head of yours?"

"I need to call work and tell them I won't be finishing out my two weeks notice," she murmured, more to herself than to him, but he nodded anyways. "And I need to cancel my plans to go out for drinks with Rachel tomorrow night."

His nod reassured her a little, "No problem. I'm going to call Rogan right now and see if they can manage the ranch for us while we're gone. There's no telling how long we'll be there."

"No!" she didn't mean to yell at him, but her fear just kind of bubbled up and out via her voice box. "I mean, you can't just leave the ranch for an unknown length of time. You should stay here, and for that matter so should Dalton and Clint. This is your life, Tanner. You—" The sour look on his face caught her off guard and she stopped speaking to stare at him in confusion. "What is it?"

"You still don't get it, Zoey. I love you. You are my life. Not this ranch, or the animals, or the ranch hands, or anything else. I will go with you to Wichita, and so will Dalton and Clint because it's our right as your men. There will be no more discussion about it, got it?"

Zoey nodded as Dalton and Clint stepped into the room and Clint picked up where Tanner left off, "Damn right, angel. We'll handle the details, you just get packed and be ready to go." He looked over to Dalton, "Can you get us a flight, while I call the school for her? It would be my pleasure to tell them she won't be coming back."

"I will get us there as fast as possible," Dalton agreed before he disappeared back down the hallway. Zoey accepted a tender kiss from Clint, and then he turned to talk to Tanner about the ranch business that would need handled while they were gone.

While they were distracted, Zoey went to her room to collect her things. Packing random handfuls of clothing without really even focusing on what she was putting in her bag. It wasn't like it would matter. Who really cared if their blouse matched their shoes and their bag while a loved one's life was at stake.

The thought of her mother being her loved one made her snort. At one time she thought she loved the woman, but after everything that had happened, it seemed almost too much for her to forgive. Even considering Eve might be dying. Guilt niggled in the back of her brain. For God's sake, her mother might be dying and she was still pissy about missing money.

The thought rattled her nerves making her drop the pouch of makeup and hygiene products she was trying to put in her bag. For some reason, seeing all of her belongings scattered on the floor, finally flipped the switch on in side of her, and she fell to her knees surrounded by shampoo, conditioner, and deodorant to have a good cry. It occurred to her that she had cried more in the last few weeks of her life than she had in the other twenty-five years. Maybe love wasn't all it was cracked up to be.

Once she had dried her tears, she completed her packing and headed for the living room to find her men. Tanner was talking to Rogan on the phone, but the moment he saw her he lifted his arm. She walked right into his embrace, relishing the smell of freshly showered man, and the comfort of his arms.

"Zoey, Rachel wants to talk to you, are you up for it?" he asked her softly, concern etching lines into his brow.

She nodded and accepted the phone. "Hey, Rach."

"Zoey, are you alright? Do you want me to come with you?"

She hesitated because for almost two decades, Rachel was the person who supported her when she needed it. Her shoulder to cry on, her sounding board, and her confidante. But her eyes landed on the three Keegan brothers who were talking quietly on the other side of the room, and she knew her point of reference had been altered.

"No, Rach. I'm good. The guys are all coming with me. You need to be at home with your family."

Now it was Rachel's turn to grow quiet. When she finally spoke there was an echo of shock in her voice, "You did it didn't you? You went and fell in love with all three of them."

Zoey made a sound of acknowledgement, but she didn't want to draw the guys' attention so she didn't fill her best friend in on the story.

"Now I'm really sorry we're not going for drinks Tuesday. When you get back I want all of the details. Even the kinky ones. But for this moment, just let them take care of you, Zoey. If I know Tanner, he wants nothing more than to be needed, and right now you need someone to lean on. Let him be your rock."

Zoey sniffled a little, "I will, and I promise I'll explain more later. Thank you, Rach."

They disconnected the call, and Zoey went directly into the center of her three men, allowing their large bodies to shield her from the fear of what was waiting for her in Wichita.

---

*I'm sorry, Mrs. Keegan.*

She never corrected the misconception that she was married. What did it matter? The three men walked with her in the halls and held her while she slept. Under the curious gaze of the nurses, they kissed her and cuddled her, comforting her as she waited for news.

*...we've done everything that we can for her.*

Forty-eight hours after landing in Kansas, Zoey had gotten the bare minimum of information out of the medical staff. Her mother was in a coma, and the situation was grim. There was permanent damage done to some of her internal organs, and the doctors had no way of knowing how bad the damage to her brain was unless she woke up. The brain function tests they had been running weren't optimistic.

*I'm sorry, Mrs. Keegan, but we've done everything that we can for her.*

Right now, she was hooked up to a ventilator, and to Zoey's eyes it seemed like a million little wires held her body here on earth. From the moment she saw her, Zoey feared Eve's body was all that was left.

In the few short weeks that they were apart, it was apparent Eve had been living a hard life and using regularly. Track marks dotted her inner elbows and small sores marred her sunken cheeks. Her dyed black hair hung limply from her head—what little there was left of it—and Zoey could count every bone in her body because she had lost so much weight.

Clint had tried to keep everyone's hopes up, but as the minutes turned into hours and then days, it was clear that Eve wasn't going to get better. Now Zoey was faced with a horrific choice.

*There is no brain activity, Mrs. Keegan. At this point, our medical team would recommend that you consider taking her off life support.*

Dalton explained it all to her in plain English, doing his best to keep from saying the words "brain dead" or "pull the plug" but Zoey knew without anyone saying them. Her mom had managed to kill herself, the way Zoey always feared she would. And yet again, she left Zoey behind to be the responsible one.

*I'm sorry, Mrs. Keegan, but we've done everything that we can for her. She's gone.*

The words wouldn't quit echoing through her brain, and a feeling of defeat and hopelessness swamped her, leaving her at an impasse. She knew that the best thing for her mother was to let her go, but she couldn't help feeling as if she was stealing her last chance to live. Her emotions bounced back and forth between anger and relief. Both scared her.

She was angry that she would never have a chance to say goodbye, or clear the air. She was angry that she had to give up her right to be mad at her mom. Her mom had stolen everything from her. Money, hope, her childhood... She had spent so many years being angry at her, and now she couldn't be because her mom wasn't going to be there to be angry at. She was angry at herself for feeling relief that she would no longer have to worry about her. There would be no more mysterious appearances or disappearances. No more reminders that she wasn't wanted.

All of those thoughts and a million more filled her head while she fought through the anguish of saying goodbye. It wasn't possible to be okay with this decision. To their credit all three men had withheld giving her their own personal opinions unless she asked directly. They had done their best to support her without swaying her one way or another, and she couldn't be more grateful. Even Dalton, who had the most knowledge about what was happening medically, hadn't tried to influence her as she fought through the cycle of emotions.

"Zoey?" Tanner's voice grabbed her attention from where she sat in a hard plastic chair staring at the gray commercial grade carpet of the waiting room. "Baby, Dr. Vincent just arrived, the nurse asked me to get you."

She took a deep breath and stood on shaky knees. Dalton stood along with her and she jumped in surprise. Was she really so oblivious to the world around her that she hadn't realized he was sharing an armrest with her? His thick fingers laced through hers and drew her hand up to his lips for a kiss.

"Where's Clint?" she asked, swallowing when her voice cracked.

His beautiful toffee colored eyes met hers as he stepped around Dalton and wrapped an arm around her from the other side. "I'm here, angel. I love you, and I wouldn't leave you."

She nodded and then faced Tanner with tears in her eyes. "I don't want to do this."

The pain on his face echoed the burning in her heart, and she could barely feel it when he pressed a kiss to her forehead. "I know, baby, and if I could change it, you know I would. I hate to see you hurting."

"I just can't let go of the fact that I'm killing my mom," she whispered into the curve of his chest.

"No! That is not what you're doing. Your mom died three days ago when she took all of those drugs. You're just letting go of her so she can be at peace." Clint, Dalton, and Tanner held her in the center of their three bodies, and she soaked in their strength and love.

When she was feeling a little stronger, she pushed them back and led the way down the hall into the ICU. The doctor joined them in her mother's room a moment later, asking if she had any questions. Once she had signed the required release forms, a nurse stepped over and began removing the IV line from her mother's arm. There was a sharp click of a switch, and then nothing. The ventilator stopped rasping air into Eve's lungs, and the monitors stopped tracking her forced heartbeat. As Zoey watched her mother slip away, a wide chasm opened in her own chest.

That was it. There was no going back. No changing her mind, or asking for a second opinion. Eve was dead.

Pain and guilt melded in her stomach making her queasy, but she refused to turn away. When the nurse and doctor left the room so she could say her final goodbye, she found herself frozen to the floor. What was she supposed to say?

*I'm sorry I just pulled the plug, mom, but you never treated me right anyways, so no hard feelings.*

Her lungs felt like they were full of concrete as she forced air into them, and whispered, "I love you, mom."

Without so much as a tear, she turned and walked out of the room, virtually cutting the last ties to her pitiful childhood that still remained.

Never again would Eve make her feel inferior, but never again would Zoey be able to hug her, or laugh over her crazy life. It was over, and now she and her men would return to Stone River so they could continue their lives while her mother lay in a box. The guilt was overwhelming.

---

The funeral was like any other, awkward and somber. The reverend did his best to make Eve sound like a pillar of society, but everyone in attendance knew the truth. Zoey saw it on their faces, and felt it in their plastic offers of condolences.

A junkie didn't deserve any better, and if Eve had been proficient at nothing else in her life, she was one hell of a junkie. Zoey looked around the masses of black but didn't see her father's tall, lean form anywhere. Knowing that he didn't even bother to show up for Eve's funeral made her feel like an orphan.

Thankfully, Rachel and her men had offered up their home for the luncheon after the service. Zoey wasn't sure she could have handled having all of those people in the Keegan home when everyone was just finding out about her and the three brothers relationship. She could barely handle the curious looks right now with everything else.

By the time people started to trickle out of Rachel's home, Zoey felt like she had been bulldozed a few times. Every muscle in her body ached

—her head being the worst. Finding a quiet corner had been impossible, until she wandered into Juliet's nursery. Just as she was beginning to relax, the little girl woke and began to fuss softly.

Needing comfort herself, Zoey scooped her up and held the baby to her shoulder, hushing her and inhaling her sweet scent deeply. "Shh, don't cry. I promise everyone is leaving now, so you can rest, Jules."

It could have been just a few moments, or it could have been hours that she rocked in the rocking chair with the baby in her arms, sleeping peacefully. All she knew was that for the first time since the phone rang with the news that her mother was in the hospital, she felt at peace.

She stared down into the angelic face of her best friend's child, thanking God that Rachel had found her happily ever after, and that Juliet would never feel unwanted. She would grow up in a home with parents who doted on her, and wanted nothing more than her happiness. In that quiet moment, Zoey prayed that someday she too would find her own happily ever after. With children that she could dote on, and give all of her heart too. Hopefully with the Keegan brothers, but they hadn't had a whole lot of time to talk since everything happened.

Like her thoughts had called out, Clint's head poked into the doorway of the nursery. "Hey, angel, oh I'm sorry, angels."

He dropped to his knees at her side and stroked his fingertip over Juliet's tiny hand. Zoey's heart clenched as the baby girl's fist did. When her eyes met Clint's he was smiling.

"Feeling any better after a time out?" he asked, and Zoey felt her eyes widen. "Oh yeah, we all knew where you were. Tanner has been guarding the hallway since you came in here, refusing to let anyone disturb you. I had money on Rachel if Juliet here started fussing because there is no way the Skipper is tough enough to take on that mama bear."

"I was a little overwhelmed," she agreed, returning his smile at the mental image of her petite best friend taking on her muscular lover.

Clint nodded, "Yeah, I figured. Everyone is finally gone, so we can head for home if you want."

She wasn't fast enough to hide her reaction from him, and he frowned at her in confusion. "What is it, honey?"

"Rachel's mom went back to Oklahoma a couple of days ago. I don't have to stay at the Triple T anymore if you guys need some space," she said hesitantly. The instant the words left her mouth she regretted them. Clint's face drained of blood and his mouth dropped open in confusion.

"Zoey, I thought—"

She shook her head, and fought to hold in her tears. "I don't know. You guys have been so standoffish, and I'm so emotional, and I just didn't know what you were thinking. Are we still a thing?"

"Oh fuck, angel. If we had known... Look at me, Zoey." He stared deeply into her eyes, cupping her cheek, "I'm so deeply in love with you, that I don't remember who I was before I fell for you. And I don't want to. Yes, we are still a thing! In fact, we three guys want us to be a permanent thing, but that's a conversation for another day when you're not so overwhelmed. Today, you're going to give me Juliet, and you're going to go out and say goodbye to Rachel and her husbands, so I can take you home and put you to bed. You need rest, and time. Once you're feeling better we'll revisit this conversation, and I have no doubt Tanner will spank your ass for ever doubting how we feel."

The tears that refused to fall for her mother in the last few days finally released as Clint followed through with taking Juliet and putting her in her crib before he enveloped her in a hug. She lost track of time, but when her tears finally slowed, Dalton and Tanner were both in the room too. All three of them held her as one, letting her fall apart and grieve.

"That's it, kitten, let it out. Don't hold it in, I know from experience it hurts even more if you do," Dalton breathed into her ear.

Tanner's fingers ran through her hair, petting her and consoling her as she soaked Clint's dress shirt with her tears. Words began tumbling out of her mouth, and she couldn't control them. "She never wanted me, but I loved her. She fucking stole money from me, lied to me, cheated me, ignored me, but goddammit, she was my mom and I loved her. I never wanted her dead, but now she is and I can't do a damn thing about it. And the worst part is that I never got to tell her about you three before she was gone. The best thing in my life and she never saw it."

Zoey heard another sob in the room and lifted her head to find Rachel wrapped in Parker and Hudson's embrace as she cried with her.

"Zoey, she loved you too." She couldn't respond to Rachel's words, all she could do was nod. "Your mom was proud of you, I know it. Any mother would be."

It was as though Rachel's words breathed strength back into Zoey's lungs, and she edged out of her men's arms to embrace her friend in a much needed hug. "Thank you, Rachel, for everything. If it weren't for you, I wouldn't have survived childhood, or been strong enough to walk away and build my own future. It's because of you, that I found these guys."

"Oh, girl, you don't have to thank me. Just seeing you find happiness is all I've ever wanted for you. Let them take you home and take care of you. We'll talk soon."

Zoey let Dalton lead her from the Brooks family home and out to his old suburban where he helped her into the front seat, even buckling her seatbelt. She felt like a broken doll. Her limbs didn't seem to be attached to the rest of her as she limply stared out the window watching Tanner and Clint climb into Tanner's old red pickup truck.

When Dalton started the truck music blared from the radio, and she let herself drift with the painfully somber song by Pink. It soothed something inside of her, as she wanted answers to some of the same questions the song asked. She realized she embodied the song's words, not broken, just bent. She would move forward, with her three cowboys at her side.

Tanner would continue to worry about the ranch, and providing financial support for his family, while Clint worried more about the emotional health of those around him, and Dalton spent his days caring for their physical forms. It was a perfect triad, and somehow she was lucky enough to fit in their center. She knew in her heart that their future would have hurdles, but who really got to walk a flawless path to happiness?

When they drove through the gates of the Triple T, she felt the heaviness leave her heart. This was her home, and these three men were her future. Flaws and all.

# EPILOGUE

"CLINT JACKSON KEEGAN, don't you dare!" Zoey threatened as Clint tried to fondle her breasts from behind. They stood at the front door waiting as Tanner parked the suburban and helped Lance and Nina Keegan from it.

"Aw, don't tell me we can't have sex just because mama and pops are here," he groaned and she giggled.

"I didn't say that, but we sure as hell aren't messing around in front of them. Now, come on, you have to introduce me." She tugged on his arm, but he just looked at her like she was crazy.

"You've talked to mama on Skype every freaking week for a month making wedding plans, and you've known her since you were a little girl. Why would I have to introduce you?"

Rolling her eyes, she looked to Dalton for help. "I just mean you have to go with me to introduce me as your intended bride, you goof. Unless you've changed your mind?"

Both men growled at her, and simultaneously pushed her out the front door onto the porch. Dalton was the first to step into his mother's embrace as she rushed the porch. "It's good to see you, Mama."

Nina had tears in her eyes when she pulled back and kissed Dalton's cheek, "My, you look so handsome. I'm glad you're home for good, son."

Clint stepped up next and accepted the same greeting before tugging Zoey forward. Nina gave her a brilliant smile as she embraced her. "Zoey Carson, you are even more beautiful in person. I can certainly see why you stole my boys' hearts."

Zoey felt a blush creep up her cheeks as she accepted a hug from Lance too. "Thank you. Did you guys have a good trip?"

Lance shrugged, "I never consider commercial airline travel good, but it was alright. The place looks great, boys. When will the remodeling be done?"

They all entered the living room, and Zoey offered drinks and cookies to her future in-laws as they took seats. Clint took their luggage on up to the apartment over the garage, while Tanner filled his father in on the remodeling plans.

Nina turned to Zoey with a bright-eyed gaze and she couldn't help but notice the similarities between her and Dalton. Nina's blonde hair was pulled back in a clip, but her dimpled cheeks and brilliant blue eyes looked decades younger than she actually was. "So, dear, are you all ready for the big day?"

"No, I still have some shopping to do. I have had to wait until last minute because Clint will sneak a peek if he thinks I have presents hidden," Zoey answered, sipping her wine. When Nina looked at her funny, she laughed, "Oh, you mean the wedding! Oh I'm definitely ready for that. All that's left is picking up the flowers and the guys' tuxes."

Nina's happiness was nearly tangible as she reached out to hold Zoey's hand. "I'm so glad you four decided to have the wedding while we're here."

"Of course, Nina, we would never have left you guys out."

"I'm just so excited to see my boys married, and on Christmas Eve no less. Tell me, what can I do?"

Zoey laughed at the woman's enthusiasm. "Figure out how to hide me from those three tomorrow, because they haven't seen my wedding dress, and I want them to be surprised when I walk down the aisle."

Her future mother-in-law nodded, "And how are you holding up, sweetie? I know this is your first Christmas without your mom."

Zoey shrugged, "Not exactly, I mean, mom and I weren't ever close.

I'm managing. The guys have kept me distracted, and so has my new job. Keeping up with the backlog of cases the State of Texas has has been a challenge. There are so many kids out there in need."

"It breaks my heart to think of them not having family to spend Christmas with. I remember wishing I could steal you away from your parents' home and bring you to spend Christmas with us, if I had known how bad it really was, I would have. You were always such a sweet child. I'm so sorry I couldn't do more to help you back then. No one should have had to live in those circumstances."

Zoey shook her head, "If you had, then everything would be different. I'm happy with how my life has turned out. I have three men who love me to death, and a family of friends. I feel extremely blessed."

"You're right. We all have to experience a little of the bad in order to accept the good with gratitude when it comes our way. Now, let's call Rachel Brooks and see if we can come up with a plan for tomorrow. Maybe you should stay the night over there tonight?" Nina's words had no sooner left her mouth, than all three Keegan brothers growled and protested. Zoey laughed as her mother-in-law took charge of the herd of men like a general, and before long, Zoey was packing an overnight bag for her best friend's house.

Tanner drove her to Rachel's against his own wishes, but Zoey promised him a reward for his sacrifice after the wedding. The next twenty-four hours passed in a blur of nervous energy and happiness.

Zoey walked down the makeshift aisle between hay bales to Carrie Underwood singing "I'll Stand By You." Tears weren't necessary to express the emotions that rippled through the foursome, as they pledged their love and loyalty in front of the glowing tree as the sun set. The glow of the fireflies was extended by the hundreds of candles and torches that surrounded the small gathering.

Rachel stood holding Juliet behind Zoey surrounded by the four Brooks brothers and Mack and Ryker Thompson. Dottie dabbed at her eyes with a tissue next to Minnie and Walt White, and Lance and Nina. There was no need for anyone else. Everyone who was important to them was there, and the moment seemed more intimate because of it.

As Zoey repeated her vows with Tanner, making them legally

married, and then pledged her commitment to his two younger brothers, she felt the cool Texas winter breeze brush over her face blowing her black hair out behind her. In that moment she knew her mother was there with her, and proud of her. For despite her own flaws and weaknesses, Zoey had managed to grow into a strong woman whose love was bigger than one person.

It was as though accepting herself allowed her mother to be at peace, and the last lingering fingers of doubt that had held her heart, released. No matter where she was in her life, she would never forget where she came from, but her past wouldn't define her future. She would begin a new life this Christmas with her new family and more love than she ever dreamed possible.

The End

ALSO BY LORI KING

**Crawley Creek Series**
Beginnings
Forget Me Knot
Rough Ride Romeo
Claiming His Cowgirl
Sunnyside Up
Hawke's Salvation
Handcuffed by Destiny

**Fetish & Fantasy**
Watching Sin
Submission Dance
Mistress Hedonism
Masquerade

**Surrender Series**
Weekend Surrender
Flawless Surrender
Primal Surrender
Broken Surrender
Fantasy Surrender

**The Gray Pack Series**
Fire of the Wolf

Reflections of the Wolf

Legacy of the Wolf

Dreams of the Wolf

Caress of the Wolf

Honor of the Wolf

**Apache Crossing**

Sidney's Triple Shot

**Sunset Point**

Point of Seduction

Tempting Tanner

www.LoriKingBooks.com

**SIGN UP FOR LORI'S FREE NEWSLETTER!**

# ABOUT THE AUTHOR

Best-selling author, Lori King, is also a full-time wife and mother of three boys. Although she rarely has time to just enjoy feminine pursuits; at heart she is a hopeless romantic. She spends her days dreaming up Alpha men, and her nights telling their stories. An admitted TV and book junkie, she can be found relaxing with a steamy story, or binging in an entire season of some show online. She gives her parents all the credit for her unique sense of humor and acceptance of all forms of love. There are no two loves alike, but you can love more than one with your whole heart.

With the motto: Live, Laugh, and Love like today is your only chance, she will continue to write as long as you continue to read. Thank you for taking the time to indulge in a good Happily Ever After with her.

*Find out more about her current projects*
lorikingbooks.com

Printed in Great Britain
by Amazon